Queer and Cozy Mysteries
© 2017 by J.J. Brass
All rights reserved.

This is a work of fiction. Names, places, characters and incidents are either the product of the author's imagination or are used fictitiously, and any resemblance to any actual persons, living or dead, organizations, events or locales is entirely coincidental.

Warning: the unauthorized reproduction or distribution of this copyrighted work is illegal.

Cover design © 2017
First Edition 2017

Table of Contents

Queer and Cozy Mysteries 1
Murder at the Office 2
Chapter One...3
Chapter Two.. 24
Chapter Three 32
Chapter Four 38
Chapter Five 43
Chapter Six 47
Chapter Seven 51
Chapter Eight 54
Small Town Scandal 61
Chapter One.. 62
Chapter Two.. 81
Chapter Three 103
Chapter Four 108
Chapter Five 112
Chapter Six 115
Chapter Seven 119
Chapter Eight 132
Chapter Nine... 139
Chapter Ten 143
Chapter Eleven.. 150
The Turkey Wore Satin 155
Chapter One.. 156
Chapter Two.. 163
Chapter Three 168
Chapter Four 174
Chapter Five 179
Chapter Six 184

Queer and Cozy Mysteries

3 LGBT Mystery Stories
By
J.J. Brass

Murder at the Office

A Mother Daughter Mystery

Chapter One

When the call came in from reception, Sharon growled unapologetically. Swiping the phone from its cradle, she asked, "Rosa, what's up?"

"You've got a visitor!" Rosa replied with a giggle.

Must be Nora surprising her with an indulgent afternoon snack from the froufrou cupcake bakery downstairs.

"Send her in," Sharon said. "She knows the way."

"Aren't you even going to ask who it is?"

Sharon sighed. "Fine. Who is it, Rosa?"

The receptionist squealed into the phone before shouting, "It's Kate!"

Sharon's heart just about jumped out through her mouth. Kate? Couldn't be. Kate didn't even return her phone calls these days. That girl would never show up at the office unannounced.

Unless there was some sort of emergency.

Or maybe it was some other Kate Sharon's mind had misplaced. A client perhaps?

Sharon asked Rosa, "Kate *who*?"

"Kate *who*!?" Rosa howled. "Your daughter Kate, of course! Lady, you've been working too hard."

Goodness, it really *was* Kate.

Excitement and apprehension wrapped their fingers around Sharon's heart as she said, "Tell her to wait. I'll be right out."

No time to check her teeth for spinach or make sure her hair was relatively tame. She wouldn't have worn such a frumpy outfit if she'd known she'd be seeing her daughter today. Oh well. Nothing she could do about it now. She popped out of her boxy little office and walk-ran through the labyrinthine hallways. She worried that if she took too long getting to reception her daughter might give up on her and jet.

Sharon took a brief moment to compose herself before stepping through the glass double-doors and into the finely-appointed reception area.

"There she is!" Rosa sang, as though Sharon's daughter were Miss America.

Fat chance of that ever happening. Just look at the girl: blonde hair dyed pink and twisted into dreadlocks. Sharon couldn't help but cringe internally. She pictured her daughter as a child: expressive eyes, sweet spirit, kind demeanor. What ever happened to that version of Kate?

Trying not to let her feelings show, Sharon wrapped her arms around her teen daughter. "Katie, honey, it's so good to see you! Is everything okay?"

"Mom!" Kate growled, struggling out of Sharon's hug. "Get your hands off me."

"I'm sorry," Sharon apologized, still clutching her daughter's shoulder. "I'm just so happy you're here. It isn't an emergency, is it?"

"No emergency."

"Your dad's okay?"

"Dad's fine, Mom."

"You didn't have a fight or anything?"

"No, Mom. We never fight. *Him* and me are nothing like *you* and me."

Those words were a dagger to Sharon's heart. Kate had always been Daddy's Little Girl, but ever more so since Kate had developed her current sense of personal rebellion. It sometimes seemed she and Kate couldn't be in the same room for more than five minutes without Sharon nagging the girl and Kate screaming obscenities. Living apart ripped at Sharon's heartstrings daily, but she knew it was for the best.

"What brings you downtown?" Sharon asked. "Did you want to go out for lunch?"

"Lunch?" Kate scoffed. "It's almost 4:30."

Sharon glanced at her watch. "So it is. Did you want to go out for a bite once I'm done for the day? Get a coffee? See a movie?"

Kate rolled her eyes. "You mean you don't have plans with Nora?"

"Not tonight," Sharon said matter-of-factly. "Nora has her sign language class on Thursdays."

"Okay, well here's the thing..." Kate unzipped her backpack, which she'd doodled unrepentantly upon with permanent marker—and which was now sitting on one of reception's white leather chairs.

Right on cue the elevator dinged and who should emerge but the big boss Min and her favourite client Gwilym: a handsome younger man dressed in dark jeans and a neat jacket. He smelled like money and looked like a model. Even Kate's jaw dropped as he entered the reception area next to Min, whose outfit was equally chic: a gold-toned sleeveless silk blouse with ruffles down the front, red skirt cut to the knee but so fitted it left little to the imagination. Her black hair was done up in a neat bun, and a circular red pendant hung on a chunky chain around her neck. It reminded Sharon of the Japanese flag. Perhaps Min wore it to highlight her Japanese heritage.

"Any messages?" Min asked Rosa.

As Rosa handed the boss a stack of message slips, Min's gaze shifted across the reception area. Staring at Kate's ripped black jeans and ratty hoodie, she asked, "Who have we here?"

"Min," Sharon said. "You remember my little girl Kate."

"Not so little anymore, I see."

Sharon forced a laugh. "No, she's grown into a young woman in her own right."

"How old are you now?" Min asked.

"Almost seventeen," Kate said.

"Almost seventeen?" Sharon chuckled. "Honey, you just turned sixteen three months ago."

Kate scowled at her mother, then turned her gaze to Min. "I like your necklace. Where'd you get it?"

Min's eyes widened as she fingered the red circle against her chest. "Oh, this? It was a gift. A gift from my husband."

"He's got good taste," said Kate.

Gwilym's brow furrowed. His lips pursed noticeably as he glanced in Min's direction.

Min noticed the client's oppressive stare and stopped touching the pendant. She folded her hands behind her back, which was a rare pose for her. Usually it was hands on hips or crossed angrily over her chest.

"I gather your visit to your mother's workplace was unplanned," Min said crisply. "Otherwise I imagine you'd have worn clothing more suitable for a business office."

Kate's face fell. Perhaps she'd understand now why Sharon complained so much about the boss. Even around the office, nobody seemed to realize how much work the boss heaved on Sharon's head. No, that's not quite true. Min's assistant Hildred knew all too well how difficult the boss could be. Same went for

Olga, the office cleaning woman. Olga had more than once been the target of Min's wrath, and always for silly things like failing to leave straight vacuum patterns on the office carpeting. Poor Olga. Poor Hildred! Poor everybody who answered to Min the Terrible.

And now Kate was seeing that dreadful side of Min.

Pulling a colourful poster from her backpack, Kate said, "My band's got a gig coming up. I'm here to make copies of the poster so we can put them up all over the city. We get paid a percentage of what they take in at the door, so we really need to get people out."

"You didn't invite me to this gig," Sharon said. "Where is it? What time?"

Kate rolled her eyes. "Don't worry about it, Mom. You don't want to come."

"My baby on stage? Of course I do!"

"Mom, I really don't think it's your kind of music."

"That's not important, honey. I want to support you. I'll be there for sure, and I'll bring Nora."

Min interrupted their mother-daughter discussion with a harsh interjection. "I'm sure your mother informed you that we do not allow office equipment to be used for personal gain."

Kate's eyes widened. "Oh. Sorry. My dad said it would be okay."

"Does your father work here?" Min asked haughtily.

"No."

"But I do," Min went on. "And, furthermore, I am the boss. What I say goes. Is that understood?"

Kate's eyes filled with tears, but that old routine didn't work on Min. "I'm sorry. I didn't realize."

"I'm surprised your mother would have allowed such an infraction."

"I wouldn't have!" Sharon jumped in, feeling like a bit of a traitor for throwing her daughter under the bus. "I'm only hearing about this now, Min. I would have told her to make the copies at home."

"We don't have a colour printer," Kate mumbled.

"Well, then, at a copy shop. Whatever."

"Colour copies cost money," Kate said.

Min replied, "Exactly."

Surprisingly, Gwilym jumped in to say, "Have a heart, Min. You were young once."

Min smirked and said, "Lies."

Gwilym pulled out his wallet and fished for cash. "How much will it cost to have them done at that place across the street? Fifty dollars? Sixty?" He handed three bills to Kate. "Here, take sixty."

"Oh, I couldn't possibly accept money from a stranger," Kate said as she plucked the bills from Gwilym's hand. "You're too kind, really."

Sharon felt in awe of her daughter's artful appropriation of the client's money.

"It's my pleasure," Gwilym said, tilting his head to get a look at the poster. "Next Saturday at the Roxie? Maybe I'll check it out."

"You should!" Kate said excitedly. "I mean, if you're into lesbian feminist punk."

Gwilym smirked. "Who isn't?"

Kate glared at her mother. "A lot of people."

Min pushed her client toward the glass double-doors. "Enough fraternizing, Gwilym. Let's go to my office and get those papers signed."

When they were gone, Kate said, "Wow! That guy looks like a movie star."

"I didn't realize you could tell a handsome man from a homely one," Sharon clucked.

"I have eyes, don't I?"

When the girl started shoving her band poster back in her bag, Sharon asked, "Why are you putting that away? You should get down to the copy place before they close. I'll come with you if you're nervous about crossing the street."

"I'm not a kid, Mom! I got here on my own, didn't I?" Kate glanced at Rosa, renowned office gossip, who seemed to be taking notes. "First can you show me your new office? I haven't been here since you worked in a cubicle."

Sharon's heart swelled, knowing that her daughter cared about her day to day life. "Sure, of course. Right this way."

Min's office door was closed as they passed by, which was just as well. Min obviously wouldn't have approved of Kate traipsing around the office in such an unbecoming outfit. Sharon knew Kate had better clothes in her closet because she'd picked them out herself, but her daughter never wore nice outfits. Kate seemed to want the world to think she was a bum.

"Here it is," Sharon said escorting her daughter into the office. "What do you think?"

"It's tiny," Kate said. "Why are there papers all over the floor?"

"That's my filing system."

"Why don't you use the filing cabinets?"

"I do. They're full."

"Doesn't your boss get mad that your office is such a mess?"

Sharon thought back to all the times Min had howled at her for keeping such an unkempt workspace. In fact, she'd been moved into an office from her cubicle so Min could close the disaster zone behind a door when clients were around.

Kate shook her head. "And you used to scream at me because my bedroom was a mess."

"I didn't scream," Sharon countered. "And your bedroom wasn't just messy—you were growing mushrooms in there."

"Mushrooms are a sustainable food source," Kate said with a guarded smirk. "Everyone should grow mushrooms in their bedroom."

Sharon smirked too. "Whatever you say. You want a cranberry juice? Or a can of pop?"

"Isn't that stuff for clients? Min'll probably beat you if she catches us stealing juice."

"Okay," Sharon said. "Well, the copy place closes at five. You'd better get your butt down there. Sure you don't want me to come?"

Kate waved a hand in her mother's direction. "Oh, I'm not going there."

"Where *are* you going?"

Kate shrugged. "Nowhere."

Sharon cocked her head in confusion.

"Do I have to explain this?" Kate asked.

"Obviously."

The girl growled and then closed Sharon's office door, tossing her knapsack on the floor. "You've got a perfectly good colour copy machine right here. Why would I go anywhere else?"

"Because Min said you couldn't use the copier. Were you not listening?"

"Sure I was listening. I just don't care."

"You don't care that your mother could lose her job because you refuse to follow the rules?"

Kate heaved herself against the closed door. "Gimme a break, Mom! You're not gonna get fired for making a few photocopies."

"Oh, you think so? Well, I'll tell you why that rule is in place."

"I don't care!"

"You may not care, but you're going to listen."

Kate covered her eyes with both hands and growled.

"Because two former employees here started moonlighting."

"Whatever that is..."

"Moonlighting: working a second job. You've never heard that term?"

"No. When is it from, the 1800s?"

"Well, there was a TV show called *Moonlighting* in the 80s."

"Exactly."

"The 80s were not the 1800s."

"If it's before I was born, it's all the same to me."

"You're getting me off-track," Sharon said. "Listen: these two employees were using company resources, including the photocopier, to build a very successful small business after hours. When Phil from IT found out about their little scheme, Min fired those two on the spot."

"But the side business was successful?" Kate asked.

"Yes, very. One was a graphic designer, the other was in sales. They built up quite a host of clients looking for design work."

"So when they got fired from here, couldn't they do their side business full-time?"

"Yes, I believe that's exactly what they did."

"Well then so what? It all worked out in the end."

"For them," Sharon said. "Not for Min."

"But I thought you didn't like Min."

"I don't particularly."

"So why do you care if people screw her business over?"

That one stopped Sharon in her tracks. She hated to agree with her daughter, but Kate had a point, there. So she changed gears: "Anyway, Min's client gave you sixty dollars for copies."

"Yeah, but if I use your copier for free, I can spend that sixty bucks on... other things."

Sharon sighed. "Katie, honey, I sincerely hope you don't plan to spend Gwilym's money on illegal substances."

Kate scoffed. "Who, me? I never!"

"Mmm-hmm..."

"Hey, wait, what's that guy's name?"

"Gwilym."

"Gwilym?" Kate cackled. "Oh my God, that's awesome."

"It's Welsh, I believe."

"It's weird. I love it. I want to change my name to Gwilym."

"It's a man's name."

"Then I'll be Gwilyma. How's that?"

Sharon couldn't help but laugh. Irritating as her daughter could be at times, Kate was a truly funny kid. If only they could have more moments of mirth and fewer headaches maybe it would be possible to rebuild the fun-loving relationship they'd enjoyed when Kate was younger. Before the divorce. Before Nora.

"If you really want to use the copier, we'll have to wait until afterhours."

Kate made a face. "What am I supposed to do until then?"

"Your homework, perhaps?"

Kate stuck a finger down her throat and faux-gagged.

"Your father sent me a copy of your latest report card, Kate. There's room for improvement, to say the least."

"School is stupid. As soon as I turn eighteen I'm dropping out."

A burst of anger shot through Sharon's body as she recalled the time and money spent on tutors and enrichment classes when Kate was younger. "You most certainly will not be dropping out of high school, young lady. You will work your butt off to get into a good university, and you will earn a degree just like we planned."

Kate shrugged nonchalantly. "Dad says I don't have to."

"There is no way your father's going to let you drop out of high school."

Another shrug. "When I'm eighteen it won't matter what you and dad say. I'll live with Grandpa. He dropped out of Grade Eight."

"Times were different back then."

"Times are different now. You can get a PhD and still end up working at a coffee house. What's the point of spending all that money on a useless piece of paper? Anyway, I'm in a band."

"What's that got to do with anything?"

"I'm gonna be a musician. I don't need school for that."

Sharon collapsed in her swivel chair. "God help me!"

"See? This is why I never talk to you. You don't support my dreams."

"That's because your dreams are idiotic!"

Kate's jaw dropped. Sharon could practically feel her daughter's teeth clenching.

"Not idiotic," Sharon self-corrected. "That's the wrong word. I should have said your dreams are... unlikely. Pie in the sky."

"Oh okay," Kate snapped. "I'll just get a degree in music appreciation, then pump out a kid and be someone's secretary for the next forty years."

A typical Kate pot-shot at her mother, but it hurt Sharon to the core. "I'm not Min's secretary."

Kate raised a brow, glancing around at the stacks of paperwork piled on the floor. "Could have fooled me."

Sharon's phone rang. She took a cleansing breath before answering. It was a client trying to track down information she was sure she'd sent in an email. She spent so long on the phone Kate actually sat on the floor and pulled a math text from her bag. When the call was over, Sharon returned emails in silence, afraid of breaking her daughter's concentration.

Around 5:30, Sharon heard a familiar voice outside her door. It was Min asking someone, "Has Sharon left for the day?"

The voice that answered belonged to Phil from IT, whose office was next to Sharon's. "I heard yelling earlier, but it's been quiet for a while."

"Her daughter was here," Min said. "They probably left early. I'll have her make up the time tomorrow."

Sharon rolled her eyes. She worked late every night. She was working late now! If she wanted to head out a couple minutes early, she was more than entitled.

Another voice piped up—that of Min's dutiful assistant Hildred. "Her door is closed. She must be gone."

Min then told Hildred, "If that's the case then you'll have to process these forms for me."

"Can't I do it in the morning?" Hildred asked. "I haven't been to a single yoga class all week."

Min said, "Very well, then." She growled under her breath and went on: "Good help is hard to find."

Phil called out, "Night, Hil."

"Don't work too late," Hildred called back.

"I'm right behind you."

Kate stared silently at the closed door, visualizing Hildred pulling her purse from the bottom drawer and changing from her office shoes to her commuter sneakers.

When silence overtook the hall, Sharon crept out from behind her desk and gingerly stepped over piles of paper. Kate quietly folded her textbook closed and set it on the floor. She picked up her poster and stood, maintaining eye contact with her mother all the while.

Sharon raised a finger to her lips and then turned the doorknob slowly.

She inched open the door and peeked into the hall.

The coast was clear.

She waved her daughter over and they slipped out of her office, closed the door, and then snuck into the copy room across the hall.

Once that door was closed behind them, Sharon breathed a sigh of relief. This was somewhat of an all-purpose room, housing a kitchenette in addition to a mailroom and storage area. Fridge, coffeemaker, photocopier, fax, postage machine—with so much heavy equipment there was a soothing buzz in the air.

"Do you think we're safe to start copying?" Kate asked her mother.

"Should be. There's a back exit through that door there, but I'm pretty sure Hildred and Phil have both gone."

"What about Min?" Kate asked. "Do you think she left?"

"Doesn't matter. Min never leaves by the back door. She's too important to set foot in the mailroom."

Kate opened the top of the heavy-duty photocopier and set the poster on the glass. "Facedown, right?"

"That's right." Sharon hovered over her daughter. "How many copies?"

"I don't know. A thousand?"

"A thousand?" Sharon hollered.

Kate raised a finger to her lips. "Shhh, Mom! Keep your voice down."

"Oh, nobody will hear us in here."

Kate tried to press 1000 on the digital copier, but the screen kept defaulting to 100. Sharon wasn't about to tell her daughter you could only program up to 999 copies at a time.

"One hundred is perfect," Sharon said, and hit the START button.

A message popped up, which read ENTER PASSCODE.

"What's your passcode, Mom?"

"Oh, no. We're not using mine. Min scrutinizes everyone's printing numbers except her own. She's paranoid about being cheated by employees."

Sharon punched in Min's printer passcode. Just as she was about to hit START, the door inched open.

"Someone's coming!" Kate squeaked.

Sharon grabbed her daughter's arm and pulled the girl into the storage closet, swiftly pulling the double doors closed behind them. Though the closet was large, it was backed with innumerable boxes of paper, so mother and daughter had to scrunch together. In that enclosed space, Sharon got a generous whiff of her daughter's various body odors.

"Jesus, Kate. When was the last time you took a shower?"

"Shh," Kate said, sitting on a stack of boxes and gazing through the gap between the two doors. "Look, it's a cleaning cart. And a cleaner."

Sharon leaned over her daughter and peeked through the gap. "That's Olga. She's Russian."

As if to prove Sharon's point, the cleaner took out her cell phone, dialled a number with speakerphone on, and proceeded to chat in Russian with the woman who answered the call. Olga set her phone on her cart and continued her conversation while she wiped down the kitchenette countertop.

The door from the office opened again. High as Kate and Sharon jumped, Olga jumped even higher. Rushing to the cleaning cart, she smacked her phone, hanging up on her friend.

"Oh. Hello," she said to the unseen figure who'd just entered the mailroom.

"Howdy, Olga."

"Who is it?" Kate whispered to Sharon.

"Sounds like Phil."

"I thought he left already."

"So did I."

The fridge opened and closed—they knew this by sound alone—followed by the crackle-fizz of a can of pop.

"You are drinking orange?" Olga asked. "You usually drink grape."

"What can I say? I feel like something a little different today."

"Ahhh."

Phil stepped into view as he took a long swig. He then held the orange can at arm's length and said, "Today is the first day of the rest of my life."

"Yes," Olga replied as Phil made his way past the mail sorting area. "Nighty-night," he said as he opened the back door and left.

Olga returned to her phone when he'd gone, but before she'd finished redialling, the office door opened once more. Olga huffed as another unseen figure entered the room.

"Oh darn. Did you dump out the coffee already?"

Olga threw her phone at the cart like it was on fire. "Yes, Miss. Did you want a cup?"

"Yeah, I was gonna drink it on the subway."

"I am sorry, Miss."

Kate strained to see through the gap in the doors, and then asked her mother, "Who's talking?"

"Sounds like Hildred," Sharon whispered. "I thought she left ages ago."

Hildred said, "Don't worry about it. I'll make a single-serve coffee at reception—just don't tell Min. She'd freak. She always tells everyone that single-serve machine is for clients only."

"Yes, Miss," Olga replied.

"But I don't care. I'm gonna make one anyway. You want one too? They're really good."

"No, Miss."

"You sure? The mocha latte is sooo yummy. It's probably ten million calories, but oh well. Sure you don't want one?"

"I am sure, Miss."

"Oh my God," Hildred went on. "You should have seen Min this one time when a bicycle courier tried to make himself a cup. She started screaming at him to get his filthy hands off her Keurig. It was hilarious. I felt bad for the guy."

"Yes, Miss."

"Min is such a miser when it comes to the office," Hildred said as she came into view: all four-foot-ten of her, in her chic modern clothes that would look little-girlish on anyone but a cool Korean. "Like, she'll spend inordinate amounts of money on shoes, but if anyone dares to brew a coffee from the client machine she goes on a murderous rampage."

"Yes, Miss."

Hildred leaned against the photocopier, and Kate gasped. "What if she hits the START button?"

Sharon clung to her daughter's shoulder. "Let's just hope that doesn't happen."

Meanwhile, Hildred ranted about how Min was always keeping her late but refused to pay her overtime. And when she wanted a couple hours off for a doctor's appointment, Min threatened to dock her pay.

"You know, sometimes I think my life would be easier if I quit this job and went back to living in my parents' basement. Sure they were strict when I lived at home, but in a lot of ways Min is worse."

"Yes, Miss."

"Sometimes I just want to throw my hands around her neck and scream, *Get your own chai latte, you mean-spirited, supercilious ingrate!* You know?"

"Yes, Miss."

When Olga made no attempt to inject her view into the conversation, Hildred sighed. "Well, I guess I'll take off. I've already missed my yoga class. Sure you don't want me to brew you a mocha latte?"

Olga nodded, smiling faintly.

Hildred sighed again, then said, "Okay. See ya." She left by the back door, which feeds into reception, the land of forbidden single-serve coffee brewers.

"So that was Hildred?" Kate asked.

"That was Hildred."

"Hmm. I always pictured her as an old woman. You don't meet many young people with a name like Hildred."

"I went to school with a Hildred."

Kate gave a breathy laugh. "Well, there you go. It's an old-lady name."

Sharon didn't find the comment as amusing as her daughter seemed to.

When Olga picked up the recycling bin, Kate asked, "She won't throw out my poster, will she?"

Sharon whispered, "No, she would never take a document out of the copier."

The cleaner resumed her Russian phone conversation as she worked at cleaning the photocopier area and then the mail-sorting section.

Kate groaned. "How long are we gonna be in here? I don't want to spend my life in the closet."

"Well, you think I do?"

Sharon breathed uncomfortably. All this closet talk danced dangerously close to a topic both mother and daughter felt fine discussing with nearly everyone except each other.

"You know," Sharon said. "Nora keeps saying we should invite you over one weekend. There's a great Indian restaurant around the corner. We could order in some butter chicken and naan and tikka masala and that chickpea dish you love so much, and saag paneer—that's Nora's favourite—and we can all just relax and watch terrible TV. Remember we used to do that? Make fun of plot holes in made-for-TV movies?"

Olga chatted loudly to her friend while Kate said, "Thanks but no thanks."

Sharon's heart dropped. "Are you saying I can't even tempt you with Indian food? That's your favourite."

"Yeah, *my* favourite," Kate snapped, loudly enough that Olga glanced around the mailroom on high alert. "Why are you suddenly stealing everything that's mine?"

"Shhh-shhh-shhh," Sharon said, cupping one hand over her daughter's mouth.

Neither mother nor daughter moved in the space of Olga's silence. It wasn't until the cleaner continued on with her conversation that Sharon heaved a sigh of relief and removed her hand from Kate's mouth.

"Your hand stinks," Kate said.

"Couldn't smell worse than your hair," Sharon shot back.

"My hair does not smell!" Kate replied, then quickly sniffed her underarms. "It's my pits. That's what smells. I stopped wearing deodorant."

"Of course you did," Sharon said, peeking through the gap in the doors as Olga wheeled her cart out the back door, probably in search of a fancy coffee from reception. Then she'd be off to the next floor of this towering office building.

Sharon sat in silence, absorbing the oppressive odour of her daughter's armpits.

"Is it safe?" Kate asked.

Sharon couldn't think who else might still be hanging around, aside from Min, who wouldn't come in here in a million years. Ever since she'd fired the moonlighting entrepreneurs, most workers who used to stay late now cleared out at five on the dot. Nobody wanted to be accused of using office resources for personal gain.

"Okay," Sharon said and opened the double doors.

Never had she taken such pleasure in being struck in the nostrils by the dusty scent of toner.

But before they could hit START on the photocopier, the machine started up on its own.

Sharon and Kate both jumped.

"Oh my God, that scared me!" Kate whispered. Lurching forward, she picked up the single sheet of paper that had popped out of the printer.

It read, in capital letters:

CHEATERS NEVER PROSPER

"What's that supposed to mean?" Kate asked.

"It means cheaters don't succeed in life."

Kate sucked her teeth. "I know what the saying means. I'm asking, like, who is this meant for? Us? Does someone know we're here?"

"Min, maybe?"

"You think she's on to us?"

"If she opened my office door and saw your knapsack in there."

"Oh, so now you're blaming me? Big surprise!"

"I'm not blaming you," Sharon hissed. "My purse is in there too, hanging off the back of my chair. She'd have seen both."

Kate smacked the START button with her palm and her posters started printing.

Sharon slapped her daughter's hand.

"Ouch, Mom! What the hell?"

"Why'd you start printing?" Sharon asked.

"We're obviously gonna get in trouble for printing the posters," Kate reasoned. "Would you rather get in trouble for something you *didn't* do?"

Sharon couldn't really argue with that logic. But she did say, "What if Min comes in to confront us?"

"You said yourself she never comes in here. This stupid little note is the confrontation."

"I don't know," Sharon said. "It's not really Min's style. She confronts things head-on."

"Fine," Kate said, slapping the CHEATERS NEVER PROSPER note down on the photocopier. "I'm sick of hiding in closets. If Min wants confrontation, let's give it to her."

"No!" Sharon hissed, but by the time she caught up with her daughter, Kate had already heaved open the door through which they'd entered the mailroom.

At full voice, Kate asked her mother, "Which way is your boss's—"

Kate stopped mid-sentence. Her eyes grew wide as she stared beyond the open door.

Sharon had never seen her daughter looking so appalled.

"Katie, honey, what is it?"

But Sharon answered that question for herself by rushing through the door and gazing down the hallway. Phil's office door was open. Out of it, like the Wicked Witch of the West, stuck two familiar legs and a knee-length red skirt.

"Min!" Sharon cried.

Kate yelped, "Mom, I think your boss is dead!"

Chapter Two

Sharon rushed to her boss's side and kneeled on the industrial carpet. Min was long overdue for a heart attack. She should have expected this to happen eventually. But when she geared up to slap Min's cheek in hopes of reviving her, Sharon realized this was no simple heart attack.

"Oh my God, Mom, her eyes! Close her eyes!"

Sharon hadn't noticed her daughter hovering so close. She simultaneously covered her boss's vacant stare and swatted Kate's legs. "Get away. Go away. You shouldn't be seeing this."

"She wasn't *my* boss," Kate replied, in a tone that sounded almost sympathetic.

Sharon kept her hand on her boss's still-warm forehead, pressing those lifeless eyelids closed with her finger and thumb. The office was utterly silent. If it wasn't for the buzz of fluorescent lights overhead, Sharon would have thought she'd lost her hearing, gone into shock. And perhaps that was true, to some extent.

"Look at her neck," Kate whispered, pointing to the upward-slanting marks that had no doubt been left by the chunky chain Min had been wearing. "And her necklace is gone. Remember the one I liked? She must have been strangled with it."

Sharon gazed fearfully at her daughter. "By who?"

"How should I know?!"

"Hildred was the last to leave," Sharon reasoned. "And she was badmouthing Min to Olga."

"But that girl's ridiculously short," Kate said, approaching the body. "Look at the pattern of bruises on Min's neck. It goes up at the back. Whoever strangled her had to be taller, not shorter."

Sharon gazed at Phil's sturdy office desk. "Maybe she stood up there."

Kate considered the desk, which was piled up with tech gear and paperwork. "If she stood on his desk she'd have messed up all that stuff. Do you think she'd have murdered her boss and then taken the time to put everything in order again?"

A faint knocking noise rang out from another part of the office, and Sharon waved down her daughter's voice. "Shhh-shhh-shhh!"

Kate froze beside Min's body, then whispered, "What?"

Sharon raised a finger to her lips and listened intently. All she could hear now was the buzz of the fluorescents. "I thought I heard something."

Kate's eyes widened the same way they'd done when she'd first spotted Min's dead body. "You think someone's here?"

Sharon almost said *maybe*, but she didn't want to frighten her daughter without due cause. She rose from Min's side and grabbed the heavy-duty long-handled stapler off the desk reserved for interns. If it came down to a confrontation with a cold-blooded killer, she'd rather be armed than not.

"Take my hand," Sharon instructed her daughter.

"Eww, no!"

"Just do it!"

Kate rolled her eyes. "Fine."

Sharon couldn't help noticing how forcefully her daughter clung to her. They were both as frightened as each other, it seemed. Not every day you discover a dead body around the office.

"You really think whoever did it's still here?" Kate whispered. "Wouldn't they want to flee the scene of the crime ASAP?"

"I really couldn't say," Sharon told her daughter. "I've never murdered anyone, myself. Never even attempted it."

"Only my hopes and dreams," Kate said wistfully.

"Shhh-shhh-shhh!"

Hand-in-hand, mother and daughter crept along the hallway, which was lined on the interior side by cubicles and on the outside by offices. Every office had its own window, its own door. Most every door was left open after Olga came through to empty the wastebaskets and recycling bins.

Because Sharon often worked late, she knew Min usually snapped at Olga to come back later in the evening and do a thorough vacuuming of the carpets.

The office building was a tall rectangle, and so their office was set up in a somewhat labyrinthine square shape with reception and elevators at its core. Sharon and Kate made their way slowly and quietly around that square, one step at a time, peeking cautiously into each office and behind every cubicle wall. Sharon was convinced she could hear her daughter's heart beating wildly, but perhaps that was her own. Hard to say, but the beat filled her ears. It was all she could hear, beyond the buzzing fluorescents, which seemed to get louder with every minute that passed.

When they reached the glass double doors that divided the office interior from the reception lounge, Kate whispered, "We've been at this forever, Mom. Nobody's here but us."

"We won't know until we've made the rounds."

Kate wrapped her fingers around the handle on one of the glass doors. "I'm making myself a fancy coffee."

"Don't you dare," Sharon hissed. "That coffee-maker's for clients only."

"Oh, give it a rest, Mom. The queen is dead."

"Long live the queen."

"Huh?" Kate gave the door a tug, but it didn't budge. She tried the other. "I think it's locked."

"Reception locks at six," Sharon said, glancing at her watch. "Wow, it's after six. We must have been in that closet for ages."

Kate allowed her forehead to drop melodramatically against the glass door.

"Don't do that, Katie. Your greasy forehead will leave a mark."

With a growl, Kate said, "So now we're trapped in here?"

"No, no," Sharon said, neglecting to whisper. Kate was right—there was clearly nobody left in the office. "We can still get out through the back door—the one in the mailroom."

"Good, because there's no way I'm spending all night with my mom and a corpse."

Sharon shuddered. "Who could have murdered Min?"

"Anyone, from the sounds of it."

Sharon looked at her daughter flatly.

"It must have been her assistant Hildred, or else that guy Phil. They were the last people to leave."

"That we know of," Sharon clarified. "Most of the office leaves through these doors here at reception."

"Wait a minute," Kate said, grabbing her mother's arm. "That print-out: CHEATERS NEVER PROSPER. Min couldn't have printed it, because I left the mailroom right away and she was already dead. There wouldn't have been time for her to hit print and then be murdered!"

Sharon's brain buzzed, but she knew what must have happened. "The system is slow afterhours. Sometimes I hit print and it takes ten or fifteen minutes for the thing to come out."

Kate didn't look convinced.

"I'll tell you what," Sharon said, to put her daughter's mind at ease. "Phil's computer has access to all the printer records."

"What does that mean?" Kate asked, sticking close by Sharon as they moved down the hall.

"It means we can see which terminal the print command came from."

Sharon held her breath as she stepped over Min's dead body to enter Phil's office. All the electronics made the room buzz, and kept it a balmy temperature even in summer when the air conditioning was going full-blast.

Her arm felt like it was about to fall off from lugging that heavy stapler around the office, so she set it on Phil's desk as she made herself comfortable in his chair.

"Maybe we shouldn't be in here," Kate said, bundling both hands beneath her chin. "This is the scene of a crime—of a *murder*—and now our fingerprints will be all over Min and all over... all over *everything*."

"It's fine," Sharon said. "I work here. The police will understand."

"Will they?" Kate asked, with unexpected gravitas.

"Sure. Of course." Sharon was concentrating more on pulling up the printer records than on her daughter's concerns. "We're fine upstanding people. We're not the murdering type."

"Speak for yourself," Kate shot back. "Cops'll take one look at me and haul my butt to jail."

"You should be arrested for crimes against nose-kind. Pee-yew!"

"Mom!" she whined. "I'm being serious right now. Oh my God! You don't even care."

"Oh course I do, honey, I'm just trying to concentrate." Sharon located the printer record on Phil's hard drive and pulled it up. "There you go. Last print demand came from Min's terminal. She must have done the CHEATERS thing to send us a message and then..."

Kate snuck a quick peek at the body. "And then what?"

Good question. "Well, obviously someone killed her."

"But who?"

As Sharon closed out the printer record, Kate watched over her mother's shoulder. When she minimized that screen, the one beneath it was his email account. Something caught Kate's eye and she pointed before Sharon could close it out too.

"Oh my God," Kate said. "Look!"

Sharon hit her daughter's hand away. "Katie! It's rude to read other people's email."

"But look, Mom! Look!"

The subject line read: CU46 D8 CX.

"It's an email from Min to Phil. So what?"

"So that subject," Kate said. "Don't you know what that means? Of course you don't. You're a million years old."

"What's that got to do with anything?" Sharon asked. "It's a file name or something."

"Mom," Kate said, sighing heavily. "I really don't think it is."

Sharon looked up at her daughter, finding Kate's cheeks unusually rosy. "Katie! Are you blushing?!"

"No!" Covering her cheeks, Kate said, "I just think your boss was having an affair with this computer guy, that's all."

"Min? And Phil?" Sharon asked. "I can't even begin to picture that."

"Just take my word for it, okay?"

"No, not okay. That's quite an allegation."

"Well she's dead now, so it doesn't matter, I guess."

"It certainly does matter if Phil was having an affair with Min. Maybe he killed her over... I don't know... jealousy or something. Maybe he wanted her to leave her husband."

Kate shoved her mom out of the way to grab the mouse and scroll through Phil's emails. When she came across more cryptic acronyms, her eyes bugged and her cheeks glowed like cherries.

"What is it?" Sharon asked. "What did that C4X thing mean?"

"CU46," Kate said, scrolling back up to it.

"Right. What is that, some kind of code?"

"Kind of," Kate replied with uncharacteristic shyness. "They're abbreviations kids use online so parents don't know what they're chatting about."

"How do you know about them?"

"Because I'm sixteen, Mom! Oh my God!"

"Calm down, already." Sharon pointed at the subject line CU46 D8 CX and asked, "What does this one mean?"

Kate pointed at the D8. "It means they had a date." She moved her finger to the CX. "But it was cancelled."

"Does it have to mean a *date*-date?" Sharon asked her daughter. "Maybe they just had a meeting and it was easier to abbreviate it as a date."

"No, Mom," Kate said, letting her irritation shine through. "Because the first part, CU46, that means *See You For Sex*. They had a sex-date but Min cancelled it."

Sharon's ears rang. It wasn't easy hearing her sixteen-year-old daughter talk about sex, much less reveal her knowledge of contemporary sexual lingo.

But they had bigger fish to fry—namely, figuring out who killed Min.

Sure most people would call the police. It's not as if the thought hadn't crossed Sharon's mind. But Kate was right: homicide investigators would surely cast their suspicions over the very people who'd found Min's murdered body. And Sharon loved her daughter, but Kate's grungy appearance wouldn't exactly ingratiate her to police officers.

Best if they figured out who killed the boss *before* calling in the cavalry.

How hard could it be to solve a murder?

Chapter Three

"We don't know for sure that Phil and Min were having an affair," Sharon said. "Their date was cancelled, right?"

"Yes, according to this email, but if we scroll down here..." Kate used the mouse to move through Phil's account. "Look: there are tons of requests."

Kate pointed out the cryptic subject headings:

FMLTWIA

EMP

FMUTA

"What do these all mean?" Sharon asked her daughter.

With a nervous chuckle, Kate said, "Trust me, you don't want to know."

"Kate," Sharon said flatly. "I'm not exactly a prude. I know what sex is."

Kate scrunched up her nose. "Yeah, but... not this kind of sex... I hope." She pointed to the one that said FMUTA and said, "Even *I* wouldn't do that."

Sharon cleared her throat. The fleeting thoughts that dusted her mind in that moment proved immensely unpleasant.

"So Phil and Min were having an affair," Sharon said in hopes of shifting the subject away from sex. "Do you think that's why he killed her?"

"Are we sure it was him who did the deed?"

"Who else?"

Kate stepped over Min's corpse, whispering "Sorry, s'cuse me."

Sharon followed her daughter into the hall.

"Her assistant was the last person to leave, as far as we can tell." Kate stood at the door leading into the mailroom. "Look. If I'm standing here, I can't *not* see the dead body sticking out into the hallway. Even if Hildred didn't kill her boss, she had to have seen those legs on the floor."

"True..."

"You think she'd have spotted her boss on the floor and just shrugged it off, then went into the mailroom to badmouth Min to the cleaning lady?"

"Also true. And Hildred certainly had a lot to say about Min tonight."

"Too much to say," Kate added. "Almost like Hildred was trying to keep Olga in the mailroom so she wouldn't backtrack into the office."

"And discover Min's corpse."

"Exactly!"

Despite the circumstance, it was nice to spend an evening with her daughter. Minimal arguments. Collaborating toward a shared goal. If you set aside the fact that Min had been murdered, this was the nicest time they'd spend together in years.

"We've already established Hildred was too short to strangle Min," Sharon said.

Kate corrected her. "Not too short to strangle Min, just too short to create that particular bruising pattern."

"Right. Well, that's what I meant."

"Uh-huh," Kate said with a smirk. "So what do you think, mom? Hildred and Phil were in cahoots?"

"They must have been."

"If Phil was a jealous lover, that's a solid motive to kill, but what about Hildred?" Kate asked. "You know her. I don't. Would she have plotted to kill her boss just because Min made her work late a few nights?"

"It's more than just a few late nights," Sharon clarified. "Min treated poor Hildred like a servant. Not just that, but Min ran hot and cold with the girl. One minute it's bestie-bestie, the next it's meet-my-slave-Hildred. That's a very confusing kind of relationship to be in."

Kate asked, "Isn't that what Min's like with you too?"

Sharon's throat closed up when she tried to produce a response. The sound that emerged was something of a choked sob. Highly unexpected.

"Sorry," Kate said. "I guess I can't talk about Min in the present tense anymore."

That thought hadn't even crossed Sharon's mind. Min was larger than life. Even the dead body... well, Sharon half expected it to stand up and dust itself off and resume life as Min the Terrible.

"It isn't possible..." Sharon began.

"What isn't possible?"

"Sorry, I'm just thinking... is it possible that Min killed herself? If she'd hung herself by her necklace, it would have left those same marks on her neck."

"Then how did she end up on the floor, Mom?"

Sharon shrugged. "Necklace broke."

"Then why aren't there piece of broken chain all over the place? And wouldn't she have fallen on her face, not her back? No, she was definitely strangled."

"Oh, that's right," Sharon said, taking a quick glance at the body she was desperately trying to ignore. "Min's necklace is gone."

"You think Hildred took it?"

"Maybe." A thought occurred to Sharon, and she rounded Hildred's cubicle, which was roughly across from her own office. Whenever she had her door open, they could roll their eyes at each other every time Min howled from the corner office.

"What are you doing?" Kate asked.

Sharon gave Hildred's bottom drawer a tug. It didn't budge.

"Hildred keeps her purse locked in this desk drawer," Sharon explained. "If she wanted to stash that necklace somewhere, this would be the location of choice."

"But it's locked?"

"That it is."

"And Hildred has the only key?"

An idea sparked in Sharon's mind. "No! The office manager has keys to every lock. Brenda keeps them in her desk and I know for a fact she doesn't lock it."

Grabbing her daughter by the hand, Sharon pulled Kate past Min's corner office, beyond the double doors at reception, and around another corner.

Kate pointed to the bathroom sign across from the office manager's terrain. "Mind if I make a pit stop?"

"Really, Kate? At a time like this?"

"I can't help it if my body has to pee!"

"Now that you mention it, I could go too. I didn't feel it until you said something."

"I didn't feel it until I saw the bathroom."

They surged into the shiny, contemporary washroom and closed themselves behind the stall doors. For a moment, all was silent.

"You go first," Kate said.

"I'm trying. It's too quiet."

Sharon could have sworn she heard a noise on the other side of the office, and it scared the pee right out of her.

"Thanks," Kate said.

Sharon didn't mention the noise to her daughter. No sense frightening the girl over some imagined sound. And if the noise had been real, it was probably just Olga returning from her other duties to finish vacuuming.

"Weird that the bathrooms are so far away from Min's office," Kate mused as they washed their hands. "You'd think she would pick an office close to all the major amenities."

"Oh, Min's office has its own private washroom," Sharon said.

"It does? I didn't notice when I poked my head in."

Sharon grabbed a paper towel. "There's a hidden door in the corner—a faux bookcase."

"Ohhh, like a secret passageway in those old Hardy Boys books dad used to read me."

"Except not a passageway—just a toilet and a sink."

"Wish I had a secret bathroom," Kate said as they stepped into the hallway.

Sharon led the way to Brenda's office and dropped into the woman's chair, knocking the keyboard and mouse in the process. As she reached for the drawer containing the office key ring, Kate gasped.

Sharon shot straight up. "What?"

"Look!"

Sharon expected her daughter to point into the hallway, but instead Kate pointed to the computer screen.

One of the office manager's most recent incoming emails had the subject line:

CHEATERS NEVER PROSPER

Sharon's heart nearly stopped when she saw that. "Oh no! Min reported us for making colour copies! I'll lose my job for sure."

"No, the email isn't *from* Min," Kate said, indicating the name in the FROM column. She opened the email and quickly said, "It's *about* Min!"

Kate had always been a fast reader. It took Sharon a moment or two to catch up. "Gosh," she said. "It's from her client Gwilym."

Reading aloud, Kate said, "It is with a heavy heart that I am forced to report your boss is a lying, cheating..." Kate hesitated before saying the word, "whore."

Sharon picked up where her daughter left off: "It has recently come to my attention that Min has been fornicating—"

"Now that's a word you don't hear every day."

"—with a member of your staff. I demand that you fire Phil from IT forthwith."

Before Sharon finished reading the email, Kate was already scrolling down to the office manager's response. Brenda basically informed the client that she didn't concern herself with employees' personal, private lives and, anyway, Min was the boss.

"There's a response," Kate said, scrolling down to Gwilym's final reply: "In that case, I will be forced to take matters into my own hands. Good day to you."

Gazing up at her daughter, Sharon asked, "What's that supposed to mean?"

"Makes it sound like he's gonna kill Phil."

"Or..."

Kate's expression fell. "Or Min."

Chapter Four

"But why would Gwilym kill Min just because she was cheating on her husband?" Kate asked. "He's really that opposed to adultery? What, is he some kind of religious zealot or something?"

"I don't think so," Sharon said, neglecting to mention how impressed she was by her daughter's ability to use the word *zealot* in a sentence.

"Then why does he care so much?"

Sharon grabbed the keys out of the office manager's drawer. "I don't know, but I've got a bad feeling about all this. Let's call the police and get out of here."

"Can't we wait until after we leave to make the call?" Kate asked as Sharon reached for Brenda's phone. "I want to shower and change my clothes before I talk to the cops."

Her daughter's self-consciousness tugged at Sharon's heartstrings. "They might think you were trying to wash away evidence."

"I don't care what they think," Kate snapped. "I just want to take a shower, okay? Is that really too much to ask?"

Sharon exhaled heavily and dropped the phone into its cradle. She jangled the keys. "Come on. Let's check Hildred's desk and get out of here."

They walked swiftly through the office.

While Sharon tried out various keys in Hildred's bottom drawer, she asked Kate, "Wait, why am I doing this?"

Kate didn't seem to hear a word as she opened the door to Sharon's office. "Mom? Mom? Mom?" She raised one hand, pointing in horror.

"What is it?" Sharon asked, racing to her daughter's side.

"Look!"

It was nothing.

Kate was pointing at *nothing*.

"That's where I left my bag," she said. "Right there. On the floor. Where'd it go?"

"I don't know, honey." Sharon glanced at her chair. "My purse is gone too."

"Mommeee!" Kate cried, swivelling on a pile of papers to hug Sharon tight. "Someone took our bags. Someone must be here!"

A chill travelled Sharon's spine, as if ice water had been injected at its base. She held her daughter, thinking guiltily how glad she was to share this moment of closeness. Though she shared Kate's trepidations, she knew every strange occurrence in this office ultimately had a reasonable explanation. More than that, the explanation was usually quite mundane.

"I thought I heard a noise down here while we were in the washroom. I bet it was Olga with her cleaning cart. She probably looked in here, saw that we'd left our bags behind, and took them down to security for safekeeping."

Sharon moved around her desk, her daughter still clinging to her as she reached for her phone.

"What are you doing?" Kate whimpered.

"I'm just calling down to security. Calm down, Katie. Everything's going to be okay."

There was a button on the office phone than rang directly down to the security desk in the lobby, but when Sharon pushed it... nothing happened.

"What's wrong, Mommy?"

"Everything's just fine." Sharon kissed Kate's dreadlocks. The scent of her daughter's scalp and hair and skin and sweat smelled as sweet to her now as it had when Kate was just a babe, when they bathed her in the kitchen sink and swaddled her in that yellow towel with the little cap on top and bear ears sewn to the sides.

Sharon hit the switch repeatedly and pressed the security button once more.

Nothing.

No ringing.

No dial tone.

Just silence.

"Someone took our stuff, Mom."

"I know, Kate."

"And I don't think it was the cleaning lady."

Sharon held her daughter tighter. "I think it's time to call the police, Katie."

Kate nodded in agreement as Sharon dialled 9-1-1.

Still no luck with the office phone. She hit the numbers, but nothing registered.

"What's wrong?" Kate asked.

"I don't know. It must be unplugged or something."

But it wasn't unplugged. It simply didn't work.

"It's okay," Sharon said. "You can call from your cell phone."

Kate reached into her back pocket, but then said, "My phone's in my backpack."

"Mine's in my purse."

They rushed from Sharon's office and took a hard right. The phone in the next office didn't work either. Same story with the one after that.

Min's office was next, but even her phone was out of commission.

"Min always has her cell on her," Sharon said. "We'll have to check... *the body.*"

"But where?" Kate asked. "You saw what she was wearing. That skirt didn't exactly have pockets."

"She'll have tucked it in the waistband of her skirt."

Kate made a face.

"Trust me."

"How do you even know that?"

Grimacing, Sharon said, "Don't ask."

Sharon stuck her head out of Min's office. She gazed intently down the hallway that led toward the washrooms, then the other way, toward Min's Wicked Witch of the West feet.

"It's so quiet," Kate said. "Maybe you're right. Maybe the cleaning lady took our stuff."

Another idea sparked in Sharon's mind: "Maybe Olga killed Min!"

"No, she couldn't have," Kate said, clinging to her mother's arm. "Because we saw Phil and Hildred leave after she was already in the mailroom. Unless they were all in on it together."

"No, no, Katie—Olga could very easily have wheeled her cart out the mailroom door and into the reception area. From there, she could have come back in through the glass double doors, circled the office counter-clockwise, murdered Min, and gone back out through reception. We wouldn't have seen her because we were still in the mailroom."

"But why wouldn't she have left through the mailroom?" Kate asked. "The door here is so much closer than reception."

Sharon knew there was only one answer: "She must have known we were in that closet the whole time."

"How?"

"She must have heard us talking," Sharon grumbled. "I told you to keep your voice down."

"Well, excuse me for living!"

"We don't have time to argue, Kate. If Olga took our bags, she knows we're still here."

"And if she knows we're still here," Kate reasoned. "Oh my God, Mom! She might come back to kill us!"

"She's certainly hefty enough to have strangled Min," Sharon said as she pulled her daughter into the hallway. "Come on. We need Min's phone."

"But you said it's tucked inside her skirt."

"That's right."

"Gross. I'm not touching your boss's dead body."

"Fine," Sharon said, quickly approaching the end of her rope. "I'll do it. You keep a look-out."

But as they approached, they were in for another surprise...

Chapter Five

Min's body remained on the floor, flat on her back, feet in the hallway, head in Phil's office—precisely where it had been when Sharon and Kate had first discovered it. But now there was a sign across her chest, a familiar computer printout that read:

CHEATERS NEVER PROSPER

Sharon froze while her daughter grabbed her arm.

"Mommy," Kate said, her voice quivering dramatically. "Who put that there?"

Over the years, Sharon had fallen for a number of her daughter's practical jokes. She needed to be sure this wasn't one of them, and so she said, "Tell me truthfully, Katie: was it you?"

Kate looked mortified, but that look could easily be faked.

"Just tell me," Sharon prodded. "I won't be upset. Did you put the note on Min's body?"

An expression of disbelief took over and Kate asked, "When would I even have done that? We've been together this whole time! I haven't been out of your sight for more than two seconds."

"Except in the bathroom."

"Excuse me?" Kate cried. "You think I somehow managed to sneak out of the washroom, run all the way back here, grab that note off the top of the printer, then run all the way back and pee before you got out of the stall?"

"It does sound a little far-fetched when you put it that way."

"Yeah, nobody can pee that fast!"

"I meant running from one end of the office to the other. You're not exactly on the road to Olympic glory, Kate."

"Thanks for those words of encouragement, Mom."

Crouching beside her boss's body, Sharon gently flipped up Min's silky top. Her smartphone was tucked into the waistband of her skirt.

When the CHEATERS NEVER PROSPER sign fell softly to the floor, Kate asked, "Who put that there, Mom? Who could have?"

"Well, it must have been Olga," Sharon said offhandedly as she struggled to remember the passcode to Min's phone.

"But *why*? Why would the cleaning lady call Min out as a cheater? Wouldn't her beef with Min be something about Min bitching at her or whatever? Why would she care if Min was cheating on her husband?"

"Maybe she caught Min and Phil together," Sharon suggested. "Maybe she walked in on them going at it in Min's office."

"Or in that private washroom I've heard so much about." Looking over her mother's shoulder, Kate asked, "What's taking you so long?"

"I can't remember her password. I know it's got M's and 4's. I never understood what it meant."

"How do you know her code?"

"Well, I've seen her punch it in enough times."

Kate's eyes widened and her brows rose. A smile crossed her face as she plugged in: MM4M.

Min's phone unlocked like magic.

"How did *you* know Min's password?" Sharon asked.

"You said M's and 4's. It could only be MM4M," Kate said with a shrug. "More Money 4 Me."

"Gracious, doesn't that just fit Min like a glove?"

"Wait, what's this?" Kate asked, pointing to the phone as Min's email account popped up onscreen.

A flurry of communications had been sent back and forth between Min and the office manager, discussing the accusatory email from Gwilym.

"This must have all been going on while we were hiding in my office," Sharon said.

"Or in the closet," Kate added. "Wait, let me look at this one folder."

Kate opened a folder called IWS in Min's email.

"What's IWS?"

"Don't worry about it," Kate said, scrolling through messages from Phil... and messages from the good client Gwilym. "Wow, Mom. Phil wasn't the only man Min was cheating with."

"How do you know?"

Kate turned the screen away from her mother. "Just... trust me. From these messages it looks like... oh my God, Mom, there are emails from Gwilym going back over a year! The ones from Phil just started about a month ago.

Sharon glanced at Min's elegant body, which actually looked quite peaceful if you didn't look too closely at her face. But that strange CHEATERS NEVER PROSPER sign lay next to her on the floor, a condemnation even in death.

"Min's client had an affair with her first," Kate went on. "Before she started sleeping with Phil."

"I never knew any of this," Sharon said.

"That's because you're naïve, but whatever. Listen: if Gwilym was having an affair with Min for over a year and then suddenly Phil's in the picture too, maybe Client Guy felt like Min was cheating *on him* with IT Guy. See what I mean?"

"So you think... you think Gwilym killed Min?"

"His email to the office manager said he planned to take matters into his own hands."

"And so he strangled Min," Sharon said, half in disbelief, half putting the puzzle pieces together in her mind. "And he printed out CHEATERS NEVER PROSPER from Min's machine."

Kate looked like she'd seen a ghost. "Gwilym's the one who put the sign on Min's body." Reaching for her mother's hand, Kate said, "But that means he's..."

"Still in the office."

No sooner had Sharon finished her daughter's sentence than the handsome client stepped out from Min's corner office wielding an industrial stapler. Sharon looked to Phil's desk, where she'd left the one she'd been carrying around earlier, but it was gone. Gwilym must have placed that note on Min's body and then grabbed the stapler to prepare...

...for his attack on mother and daughter!

Chapter Six

"Very good," Gwilym purred as he began his slow approach. "Took you long enough to figure it out, though."

Kate swivelled to face the client. "Oh my God! Where did you even come from?"

"The one place Hen and Chick didn't think to look," he replied.

Kate said, "Min's private bathroom."

"It's been the site of many a happy tryst," Gwilym replied.

Scrunching up her nose, Kate said, "Thanks for sharing."

Sharon clutched her daughter to her chest, but as she began to step back she nearly tripped over Min's unyielding leg.

"Watch your step," Gwilym chuckled. "Don't want to end up flat on your back like your boss, there."

Sharon wasn't sure precisely what the client meant by that, but she in fact took it more as a threat against her daughter than herself. That's why she whispered in Kate's ear, "Call the police and get ready to run."

Kate nodded almost imperceptibly and clutched Min's phone to her chest as she dialled.

"You figured it out," Gwilym went on as he continued his measured approach. "I was Min's one true love. Her husband meant nothing to her. She never cared for him."

"9-1-1," the operator said, her voice muffled by Kate's top. "What is your emergency?"

Hoping Gwilym hadn't noticed the call her daughter had placed, Sharon said, "Maybe Min didn't care for her husband, but she did care for Phil. That's why you killed her. She fell in love with someone new."

"No!" Gwilym howled, whacking the stapler against the wall so hard he drove a hole through the sheetrock. "Weren't you listening? *I* am Min's one true love. *Me*! Not her husband. Not Phil."

"Min had a wandering eye," Sharon said, provoking him for the sake of the 9-1-1 operator listening in. "She couldn't commit to you any more than she could to her husband."

Gwilym got a mean glint in his eye as he looked at Sharon. "You would know better than anyone."

Kate turned slightly. "What's he mean by that, Mom?"

Sharon shook her head. "We worked closely together. I knew Min well."

"Well enough to realize her phone would be wedged inside her skirt," Gwilym said, as if that knowledge carried some special meaning. "And how would mousy, middle-aged Sharon—who left her husband *for another woman*—know a thing like that?"

Kate's expression tumbled. "Yeah, Mom. How *did* you know?"

"I've seen her shove her phone in the waistband of her skirt a million times," Sharon said defensively. "Min doesn't like pockets or purses. So what?"

"So I heard what you said earlier," Gwilym said, getting closer as he wielded that huge metal implement. "Your daughter asked you how you knew and I heard you very clearly say: *You don't want to know*. Those are damning words, dear Sharon."

"They're not," Sharon pleaded, more for Kate's sake than the client's. "I just meant Min would sometimes… cripes, do I have to tell you this?"

Kate's voice quivered as she said, "I really think you should, Mom."

Sharon swallowed her pride and said, "Sometimes we'd be talking in her office—about business matters! All business—and she'd have to... relieve herself... so she'd go into her private bathroom and... well, she'd keep talking, keep the conversation going."

"Eww, you mean she'd pee in front of you?" Kate asked.

"She always placed her phone on the counter so it wouldn't accidentally fall in the toilet."

"But, let's get this straight," Kate said. "She didn't close the bathroom door?"

"Oh, it's not such a big deal," Sharon said, feeling her feathers very ruffled by all this. "Men do it all the time, continue their conversations at the urinal."

"How would you know?" Kate asked.

"Well, I don't *know*. I just *assume*. Anyway, it's all perfectly innocent."

Gwilym slammed the heavy-duty stapler against the wall once more, putting another hole alongside the first. "Enough lies! You're as much of a cheater as Min. You have a wife at home. How *could* you?"

Stepping out from behind her daughter, Sharon said, "See here, young man: first off, I'm not actually *married* to Nora. Not yet, at least. We've talked about it, sure, but we wonder if—"

"Mom!" Kate hollered.

"Right. Sorry. And second of all, I resent the implication that because I love one woman I would jump into bed with just anyone, much less my own boss! Min and I are close because we work

49

so closely, not because we have any sort of extracurricular relationship."

"You tell him, Mom!" Kate cheered.

With renewed pride, Sharon said, "And third of all, I did not leave my husband for another woman. We were already divorced when I started seeing Nora romantically. It was a whirlwind, sure, but I never cheated. That one's more for my daughter than for you, Gwilym, because I want her to respect me."

"I do respect you, Mom," Kate said quietly. "You thought I didn't?"

"Well, it's hard to tell sometimes."

"This is all very sweet," Gwilym interrupted in a tone both saccharine and mocking. "It's almost a shame I have to kill you."

"No!" Sharon cried. "Wait! I have one more point to make."

The client only let his guard down for a second, but that's all the time it took for Sharon to raise one foot high off the ground and then slam it down on Gwilym's knee.

Kate winced noticeably at the sound of bones cracking. Soon the hallway filled with the client's cries of both pain and surprise. He obviously hadn't seen that one coming.

Sharon didn't wait around to see what would happen next. Pressing her daughter down the corridor, she shouted, "Now! Run!"

Chapter Seven

As they leapt over Min's legs and rounded the corner, Kate hit speakerphone and asked the 9-1-1 operator, "Are you still there? We need help! He's gonna kill us!"

"I'm here," the operator replied.

"This way," Sharon whispered, tugging her daughter toward accounting. "There's a fire exit into the stairwell."

Meanwhile, her daughter told the 9-1-1 operator, "His name's Gwilym and he's a client and he killed my mom's boss. Actually *killed* her! We're high up in an office building, on the 18th floor. Send the police, please!"

Kate gave the operator the street address in case they couldn't triangulate the location from cell phone towers like in TV crime dramas. Hopefully they'd be able to burst into the stairwell before Gwilym caught sight of them.

Except when they reached the alcove that led to the staircase, they met a wall of bankers' boxes. Accounting must have run out of room for filing, because they'd stacked boxes floor to ceiling, filling the entire alcove.

"This has got to be a fire hazard," Sharon grumbled.

"Where's the exit?" Kate asked.

As Gwilym limped around the corner at the far end of the hallway, Sharon grabbed her daughter's arm. "Come on. We'll have to get back to the mailroom and leave that way."

"Please get here fast," Kate begged the 9-1-1 operator as they raced past the staff washrooms, past the office manager's domain. "He killed Min. He'll kill us too."

"Get out of the office," the operator encouraged them. "Police will be there any minute."

Kate stopped briefly to tug on the glass double doors at reception. They didn't open, of course, and Sharon noted a streak of anger resonating through her chest as she grabbed her daughter and pulled her along the hall. "I told you those doors lock at six!"

"I was just checking! Oh my God, Mom! Everything I do is wrong!"

They rounded the next corner fast, but not fast enough.

Sharon figured Gwilym would have chased them around the entire office, but of course not! He was too smart for that. He'd backtracked, waiting for his prey in Min's corner office

As they ran by, he leapt out shouting, "Gotcha!"

Sharon really must have done a number on his knee, because he didn't get a perfect jump on them. But he did surprise Kate enough that she screamed and dropped Min's phone on the floor.

When she stopped to pick it up, Gwilym reached for her dreadlocks, but Sharon reached for her arm—and Sharon reached faster. "Just leave it, Kate! The police are on their way. We don't need the phone."

In Sharon's grip, Kate stumbled toward the mailroom. Mother opened the door and launched daughter through. They both raced for the elevators.

"Where do you think you're going?" Gwilym threatened, having caught the mailroom door before it closed. "You'll never get away from me."

"Yes we will," Sharon said, tightening her grip on her daughter's arm. "Don't listen to him, Katie."

Sharon pushed open the door that landed them in reception. Elevators to the left. Wonder of wonders, there was a cab sitting right there waiting for them! They sped into it and Sharon hit the Door Close button while Kate pushed L for Lobby.

The doors closed while Gwilym clattered through the mailroom and into reception.

"Oh, thank God!" Sharon said, clutching her daughter to her heart. "We're safe, honey. We're going to be just fine."

After returning a heartfelt hug, Kate looked up. The number 18 was lit up on the digital screen over the elevator doors. "Mom, we're not going anywhere."

"Oh, that's right," Sharon said. "It's after six. I need to swipe my keycard to get the cab moving."

She reached for her purse before realizing... oh dear... she didn't have her purse. No purse meant no keycard meant no escape.

"What's wrong?" Kate asked as the doors began to open. "What's happening?"

Gwilym stood outside the elevator, holding the doors open while wielding a mighty stapler over his head. "Heeere's Johnny!"

Chapter Eight

When Sharon glimpsed that crazed look on Gwilym's face, she hit the Door Close button yet again. The elevator responded immediately, but so many other things happened in that instant she felt as though she were seeing her life in snapshots:

With a gap of only a few inches between the elevator doors, Gwilym launched forward, wielding the industrial stapler like a hammer, doing his utmost to strike mother and daughter.

Simultaneously, Kate launched herself at the control panel, throwing her whole body against the big red emergency button.

The mechanisms must have jammed, because the elevator doors locked in place, trapping Gwilym's arm between them.

"I don't think that's supposed to happen," Sharon said over the alarm bells.

Gwilym laughed maniacally. "Maybe I'll sue!"

Neither Sharon nor Kate released the buttons they were holding. The last thing they wanted was for those doors to open. Gwilym would kill them both with his bare hands.

Out of nowhere, Kate asked, "It was the necklace, wasn't it?"

Gwilym's laughter stopped on a dime. "How did you know?"

Sharon whispered, "What are you talking about?" but Kate disregarded her mother's question.

"I saw the way you looked at Min when I complimented her necklace: like someone had punched you in the heart. And Min looked pretty shifty too. She said her husband gave it to her."

"Had to be a lie," Gwilym replied biliously. "Her husband never gives her jewellery. That's one of the many things she resents about him."

"But you didn't give her the necklace either," Kate went on. "And if she'd bought it herself she would have just said that. So if the necklace wasn't a gift from you and it wasn't a gift from her husband..."

"I knew she must be cheating on me."

"But how did you know with whom?" Sharon asked.

Twisting his arm relentlessly between the elevator doors, Gwilym said, "I confronted her about it. Min might be a cheater, but she can't be bothered lying. I asked her who it was and she told me."

"That's when you sent those emails to Brenda the office manager, calling them out, telling her to fire Phil."

"I sent that note from the lobby bar downstairs. I couldn't stay up here in the office, but I couldn't go far."

"And when you got the response that there would be no repercussions, you came back up to take matters into your own hands."

"Rosa at reception was packing up to go home. She told me I'd just missed Phil, but Min was still in her office. I went in through those glass doors and straight to Min. I apologized and she bought it. I told her I craved her and she believed that too."

"You waited until everyone had gone," Kate continued. "Hildred, Olga the cleaning lady... but you didn't know me and my mom were still hanging around."

"If I knew that I'd have killed you too!" Phil cried.

"Yeah right," Kate shot back. "You're too much of a wimp to kill three people. You couldn't even look Min in the eye while you strangled her. You had to stand at her back."

"That's how you strangle someone! Don't you know anything?"

"Don't provoke him," Sharon muttered.

Kate ignored the advice and asked, "How did you get her into Phil's office?"

"That's the best part," Gwilym replied. "I didn't have to. She said she needed to grab some paperwork from his desk and I just followed along. Perfect place to kill a cheater: in her secret lover's office!"

After pressing her thumb to the Door Close button for so long, Sharon started losing feeling in her digits. When the cab started trembling, she wondered if she'd accidentally released the button. But wait... she heard motion. "Are we moving? What's going on?"

It took a moment for Sharon to make sense of the noise: it was an elevator coming to a halt beside them, then the ding of a bell as its doors opened, and then a number of people pouring into the reception area.

The police!

"Arrest him!" Sharon called out. "He killed my boss! He told us so!"

Gwilym responded by telling police, "Stay back! I'm armed!"

Kate raised one heavy boot in the air and kicked the stapler from his hand. "Not anymore he's not!"

Sharon couldn't help feeling proud of her daughter. That was a brilliant move.

When she could see officers through the gap, she released the Door Close button. Police secured Gwilym quickly, cuffing his hands behind his back as he wailed that it wasn't his fault—he'd been cheated on. Any man would do what he did.

Kate responded with a full-body shiver. "Remind me never to fall for a dude."

"They're not all bad," Sharon mused. "Your father, for instance. He's a good man, always was. Even if I *had* started seeing Nora while we were married—which I didn't, by the way—he would never have reacted like this."

"True."

They stepped out of the elevator, aided by a female officer. After the paramedics had asked them if they were injured or in need of medical care, the officer asked them to go over the evening's events. They told their story so many times they could have written a book about it.

"I'm exhausted," Kate said as they sat together in the white leather reception chairs.

By then, the people from the medical examiner's office and crime scene investigation had tramped into the office to see to Min's body and collect evidence for the inevitable trial. Sharon's purse and Kate's knapsack had been found tucked away in Min's private bathroom, where Gwilym had been hiding out most of the evening.

"I think we more than deserve a mocha latte," Sharon said, setting up the client-only machine to prepare them each a flavoured coffee. "Anyway, it's not like Min'll yell at me about it."

"Ever again," Kate said as the first coffee brewed. "If the company belongs to Min and Min's dead, does that mean the company's gonna close? Are you gonna lose your job?"

Sharon hadn't thought that far in advance. "It'll depend, I guess, on how she's set things up, legally. We'll just have to wait and see."

When the first mocha latte had brewed, Sharon handed the white mug to her daughter and started brewing another.

She knew Kate hated hearing touchy-feely things like this, but she had to confess: "Tonight's been terrible in so many ways, but it's also been nice spending time with you."

Kate rolled her eyes and said, "Mo-o-om!" She took a sip of her coffee, then smirked. "But I know what you mean."

"Oh honey," Sharon said. "Why can't we get along?"

"Moms and teenagers never get along. It's the law."

"There's more to it than that. It's ever since I left your father."

"That's not true!"

"Fine, then ever since I moved in with Nora."

Kate stared into her coffee as the machine burbled away.

"Why?" Sharon asked. "I thought you'd be proud of your mother. You're certainly proud of yourself—of being a lesbian, I mean."

"Well, exactly," Kate said without meeting her mother's gaze. "It's like... I was a lesbian *first*. I came out to you and dad when I was twelve! And then after you guys get divorced you start dating a woman too? It's like you're trying to copy me or steal my identity or something. Why can't I have anything that's just mine?"

"Honey, to be fair, falling in love with a woman isn't something that's exclusively yours. There are plenty of lesbians in the world."

"Yeah, but why do you have to be one of them?" Kate slammed her coffee cup on the glass table and burst out of her chair, circling the reception area angrily. "You're trying to be all young and hip and it's *so obvious*! Why can't you just be a boring old lady? That's what a good mom would do!"

Sharon's mocha latte finished brewing, but she didn't have the wherewithal to grab it. "I don't understand this, Kate. You think I'm only living with Nora to be... cool?"

Kate covered her eyes and growled.

"Because if that's what you believe, honey, you are way off. I *love* Nora. I loved your father too—in fact, I'll always love him in one way or another—but Nora's not some kind of fashion accessory. I love her. I really do."

Kate's hands slipped down her face, leaving an expression of disbelief in their wake. "You really love her... *for real?*"

"Of course I do. You think it's easy coming out of the closet at my age? Even coming to terms with my feelings myself... well, it wasn't simple or straightforward. To be honest, it's something I really wanted to talk to *you* about. But you wouldn't return my phone calls, so..."

For a long moment, Kate simply stared at the white mug in the coffee machine. Then she circled the coffee table, picked up the mug, and handed it to her mother. "Your mocha latte is ready."

Sharon took the mug from her daughter and sipped the warm chocolatey coffee. "Mmm. It's good."

"Yeah, I like it too." She sat again in the same chair she'd been in when Sharon met her earlier that afternoon—though it felt like days ago after all they'd endured—and picked up her half-drunk coffee. "Maybe you and Nora should get one of these machines. Then when I stay over I can make myself coffee in the morning."

"Does your father let you drink coffee every morning?" Sharon asked. "Because I'm not sure how I feel about my sixteen-year-old daughter—"

"Mom!" Kate growled.

Sharon smirked, and inhaled deeply the scent of coffee and chocolate. The evening had been too tragic to think about, but intense experiences—like being chased around an office by a murderer—had the ability to bond two people, and it had certainly done so tonight.

"Katie?" Sharon said softly across the lip of her coffee cup. "I just wanted to tell you..."

Kate looked up from her coffee with an unexpected softness. "Yeah, Mom?"

"I just wanted to say..." Holding her mug a little tighter, Sharon said, "You should really go back to wearing deodorant, honey."

"Mom!" Kate slammed her mug on the coffee table. "Oh my God, you are so annoying!"

"I'd rather be annoying than smell like a zoo."

Kate sat low in her chair, both arms crossed over her chest. "I can't believe how irritating you are."

Sharon reached over and gave a playful tug to her daughter's dreadlocks. "It's my job to be irritating. I'm your mother and I love you."

Kate teasingly tried to bite her mother's hand, and snickered when Sharon jumped, nearly spilling coffee over the sides of her cup.

Rolling her eyes, Kate said, "I love you too."

"Awww," Sharon said, hand to heart, pretending those words didn't generate an instant lump in her throat.

"You're my mother. I *have to* love you."

Sharon patted her daughter gently on the thigh. "That's good enough for me."

The End

Small Town Scandal

A Queer and Cozy Mystery

Chapter One

Don't ask me why I spend three hours a week checking in on Agatha Vanderjadt. Sure she was my elementary school teacher three years running, but I didn't like her then and I don't particularly like her now. That's a terrible thing to say about a feeble old woman. In fact, it's not the kind of thing I go around saying. But it *is* the kind of thing I think quietly to myself on frequent occasion.

Agatha never locks her door, so I walk right in every Monday, Wednesday and Friday after my shift at the kennel.

Usually when she hears the door open, she shouts out, "Don't even think about tracking those muddy boots across my clean carpet!" So I kick off my boots walk up the stairs into her split-level living room to find her sitting in her easy chair, yelling at Judge Judy defendants.

First thing I ask is whether she's eaten that day.

She usually waves dismissively, then tells me I smell like dog.

So I fix her a meal and set it on the TV tray.

If I make tuna on toast, she'll say she wanted grilled cheese.

If I make grilled cheese, she wanted spaghetti.

Suffice to say it's a thankless job.

Anyway, that's what *usually* happens when I arrive at Agatha's house.

That's not at all what happened last Friday...

I opened the door and there was no mention of muddy boots. No Judge Judy blaring from the living room. *Oh God*, I thought, *she's fallen and hit her heat! She's had a heart attack! She's finally succumbed to age!*

That's why I trotted up the stairs without bothering to take off my boots.

Agatha wasn't dead, but I'd never seen her so ghostly. Her skin looked grey as she hovered over the mail, which was laid out across a lace-patterned oilcloth on her dining room table.

She barely glanced up as I approached, which was odd. Usually, she told me to keep out of the dining room. She was convinced I'd somehow manage to knock over the curio cabinet. I was a bull and this was her china shop.

"Agatha?" I asked. "You okay? You don't look so good."

She looked up at me like she hadn't even realized I was there. Her eyes seemed more sunken than normal. They usually had a sharpness to them, like you see in a dog with a mean owner, but Agatha looked strangely helpless as she pressed her arthritic hands on a stack of folded-over photocopies.

After a moment, she said, "Chris—you're a queer, right?"

Any other day I'd have taken that question for one of Agatha Vanderjadt's trademark jibes, but there was something different about her that day. So I just said, "Queer in more ways than one."

"Good," she said decisively. "Then you can help me with this. I wouldn't ask anyone but you."

"That almost sounds like a compliment."

She ignored my comment, stared right through me.

"Help you with what?" I asked.

Issuing a deep sigh, Agatha removed her hands from the papers she'd been covering. "Someone sent this in the mail. I don't know who. They didn't sign the note."

Agatha sat back in her stiff dining room chair. She folded her hands in her lap and stared at them, looking the way I'd always felt when she'd scolded me in school.

I picked up the stack of grainy photocopies and flattened them against the table. At first, I couldn't make sense of what I was seeing. I carefully sat down on one of Agatha's dainty chairs, half convinced it would snap in two beneath me. I got closer to the paper, but I still couldn't figure out what I was looking at.

Agatha must have sensed my confusion, because she reached across the table and spun the papers around.

I'd been looking at them upside-down.

"Holy Moly," I said, glancing from the image on paper to the woman across the table. "Is this what I think it is?"

Agatha nodded gravely, exhibiting a sense of shame I'd never seen from her in all the years we'd known each other.

"Which one's you?" I asked.

She pointed to the dark-haired woman, which was hard to reconcile with the white-haired lady before me.

All I could say was, "Wow."

I looked at the next image, and the next, and the next. They weren't exactly shocking, not by today's standards, but it was definitely weird to see my former teacher in such a compromising position. In a variety of compromising positions, I should say.

Stranger still to imagine Agatha Vanderjagt as a young person. Cameras must have just been invented when these pictures were taken. I wondered how long they'd had to hold each position.

"There were rumours at school," I said. "Maybe that's why I always felt a sense of allegiance with you. Even when you were mean to me, I knew we were cut from the same cloth."

Agatha raised a dubious eyebrow. "What are you talking about? We're nothing alike."

Good old Agatha.

The old woman went on to say, "All my life I've worn skirts and dresses like a proper lady."

"Yeah, well, I was never much good at being a girl—even when I tried." I couldn't help myself. I said, "Although, Agatha, I notice you're not wearing a skirt or a dress in any of these pictures. You're not wearing anything at all!"

Her lips pinched with ire, but her shoulders fell just as quickly. "Please don't judge me too harshly. You're bearing witness to a youthful indiscretion. I was very young when those pictures were taken."

"Yes, I can see that."

She'd have barely been twenty, by my estimation. Same went for the blonde woman who also appeared in the photos.

"Where did these pictures come from?" I asked.

"That, I couldn't say." She handed me the envelope they'd arrived in, but there was no return address—only Agatha's name and address printed directly on the front.

Agatha handed me something else, too: an unsigned blackmail letter demanding a not-insignificant amount of money in exchange for the original photos and the writer's discretion.

"You're not going to hand this money over," I said to Agatha.

"I have to," she said in return. "You read the note. If I don't pay up, this person will tell the whole town I'm a..." She looked all around, as though there were someone else in the house who might hear us. Bending across the table, she said, "They'll tell everyone I'm a *queer*."

"So what?" I asked with a shrug. "I'm queer and everyone knows it."

"That's *you*," she said. "You're young. It's different. And you didn't spend forty-some-odd years of your life as a schoolteacher."

"What's that got to do with anything?"

"It's got *everything* to do with anything! Schoolteachers are held to a higher degree of scrutiny than people who work at a kennel."

I had to admit she was right about that. "But you're retired. What are they going to do, fire you retroactively?"

"Not fire me, no, but revoke my pension, possibly."

"I very much doubt that."

"You're young," she said. "You don't know how older people think. Young minds are malleable. Old people are set in their ways—I should know."

"Who cares what people think?"

"I care!" she said, hissing the words like an angry cat. "If the whole world knew about my sordid past, they might think I swayed my students in a certain direction."

"Agatha," I said, trying not to laugh. "Kids can't be indoctrinated into queerness."

"But look at you," she said, in a begging tone I'd never heard from her. "You're about the queerest they make 'em, and here you are, coming to my house, fixing me dinner, helping me out. People might think..."

"That we're lovers?" I asked.

Agatha's eyes bugged. "What? No! Get your mind out of the gutter."

"Sorry! People might think what?"

The old woman let her head collapse into her hands. "They might think I *made* you this way. I converted you. After all, I was your teacher three years running."

"Nobody would ever think that, Agatha. I'm queer because I'm queer, not because of anything anyone did or said."

"The schoolboard isn't as open-minded as all that. They can't find out about my past."

Agatha's intensity made me feel for her, even if I thought she was overreacting.

I could see her hands shaking and I asked, "Have you eaten today?"

She gave me the usual brush-off.

"How's about I make us a couple grilled cheese sandwiches and we'll talk this over?"

"I'd rather have tomato and cheese."

I got up and checked her fridge. "There's no tomato."

She sighed. "Very well, then. Grilled cheese will have to do."

Instead of bringing our sandwiches to the dining room, I set them on the kitchen table. She'd been staring at those photocopies the whole time I was cooking our meal, and I wanted to get her away from her worries for a minute or two.

Easier said than done.

Agatha stared out the kitchen window as I ate my grilled cheese. Obviously the blackmail was weighing on her mind, but I knew she'd function better after she'd had something to eat.

"It's not the end of the world," I said. "Even if the whole town and the entire schoolboard gets wind of this, life goes on. Look at me. I'm queer as they come and I've got a bunch of friends, a job I love..."

"Didn't your parents disown you?"

Ouch. Low blow.

"They didn't *disown* me," I said, sitting up a little straighter. "They just said they'd never acknowledge me as their son. It's not like they stopped inviting me for Christmas or anything. Only...

they write *Christie* instead of *Chris* on my presents. And they still send *To My Darling Daughter* birthday cards."

Agatha gazed at me flatly. "If you live your life as a man but your parents won't stop calling you their *little girl*, isn't that the same as disowning you?"

"No," I said, on impulse, because I didn't want to think about the question. "Anyway, we've got bigger fish to fry. You've got this blackmailer to deal with."

"Don't remind me," she moaned.

She picked up her sandwich and took a bite, so I counted that as a win.

I'd nearly finished mine.

"Who could have done this, Agatha?"

"I don't know. I don't care. I'll just pay the money, like it says in the letter."

"You're going to leave all that cash in the abandoned mill just outside town?"

"It'll wipe out my savings, but what choice do I have?"

"You have the choice to say no."

Agatha gave me a hard look, like she wasn't going to have this discussion again.

"Okay, fine," I said. "So you hand over every last cent of your savings. Then what?"

"You read the note," she said, pointing her sandwich at the dining room. "This fellow, whoever he is, will mail me the originals and keep his mouth shut."

"And what if he doesn't?"

Agatha's eyes widened, like the thought hadn't occurred to her. "What do you mean?"

For a jaded old broad, Agatha could sure be naïve. So I said, "What if he doesn't send the pictures? What if he sends another note instead, asking for more money?"

"Well, I don't have more money," Agatha said, like that was that, problem solved.

I rubbed my face, forgetting that my fingers were slick with grilled cheese grease. I got up and grabbed a paper towel and Agatha said, "Only use half a sheet. That stuff doesn't grow on trees."

"Well, actually, it does."

"But money doesn't, and you're not the one paying for my paper goods."

I reached into my pocket, pulled out a nickel, and slammed it on her kitchen table. "That should just about cover it."

She harrumphed, but eventually softened. "You really think the blackmailer would cheat me like that?"

"I really, really do." Pacing the room, I said, "Agatha, who would do this to you? Let's confront them, you and me. Or just me. You don't have to come along, just tell me who you suspect."

"I've already told you I don't know. I wasn't the kindest of teachers—a point to which you can certainly attest. And I've taught hundreds of students over the years, so take your pick."

"Yeah, but what kind of kid is going to carry a grudge against a teacher all the way into adulthood? No, it's got to be someone from your personal life." I made my way back to the dining room and spread the risqué photocopies across the table. "You've got to admit, these are nice pictures. You had a smokin' bod back in the day."

Agatha swatted at me from the kitchen. "That's pervert talk."

"Hey, I'm not the one starring in my own series of vintage lesbian pornography."

The old lady munched sullenly on her sandwich.

"What about her?" I asked, holding up one of the photocopies and pointing to the blonde playing opposite my former schoolteacher.

"What about her?" Agatha shot back.

"Well, who is she, for starters?"

"Never you mind."

I tried not to roll my eyes, but I couldn't help it. "Agatha, I can't help you if you don't come clean. Was she your girlfriend?"

"No!" Agatha cried. "We didn't... we wouldn't have used that term."

"But she was your *lover*."

When Agatha said "Obviously," she sounded almost like a teenager.

"Was your relationship purely... physical?"

Agatha didn't answer right away, but when she did, she said, "We shared a love unlike any other I've known. If ever I'd felt that way about a man, I'd have married him in a heartbeat."

"Let me guess: she *did* feel that way about a man. And she married him and they lived happily ever after."

With a wistful laugh, Agatha said, "Martha was already married when I met her. Who do you think took the photos?"

I hadn't actually thought about that part. "Are you saying this woman's husband was the photographer?"

Agatha didn't respond, but I knew I had my answer.

"Have you kept in touch with this Martha woman?"

Agatha shook her head. "They moved away soon after their second child was born. Josef received a job offer he couldn't refuse, and that was basically the end of it."

"So let's start with the obvious suspects," I said. "Martha and—you said her husband's name was Josef?"

"Right you are."

"Do you think they would blackmail you? After all this time? I'm assuming these photos were in their possession."

Agatha shook her head resolutely. "Couldn't be them."

"You never know. If they're as old as you are, maybe they have to go into assisted living. Those places ain't cheap."

"No, you misunderstand," Agatha cut in. "It couldn't be them because they're both dead."

"Oh."

"Martha died more than a decade ago, Josef just a few years later."

"Agatha, I'm sorry."

She waved dismissively. "It's not your fault. People get old and die. That's how it goes."

So much for the obvious suspects.

"You said they had kids," I prodded. "Is that who would have inherited all their stuff?"

Agatha shrugged. "I suppose so. As I say, I haven't kept in touch."

"Do you at least know where Martha and Josef moved to?"

"Well, sure."

"Do you remember their children's names at all?"

She looked at me flatly. "It was nigh on sixty years ago they moved away."

I moved her half-eaten grilled cheese out of the way and flipped one of the photocopies over in front of her. There were pens all over the place and I put one in her hand. "Don't think. Just write: Martha, Josef, their children's names, where they moved to…"

Agatha seemed dubious at first, but it worked. Once she'd freed up her mind, the information poured out easily. We had a town to start from and children's names to work with.

"Perfect," I said, grabbing one of her five million phones. She had at least two in every room, so she wouldn't have to go far to pick up. Not that anybody ever called her.

"You're not phoning long distance, I hope."

"Think of it this way," I said. "It's cheaper to spend a few bucks on long distance than pay out your life savings to a blackmailer."

She grumbled, of course, but by then I'd already called the operator. I looked at the names Agatha had written down and inquired after the oldest child first: "Hi there. I'm looking for the number of an Eva Opavova in the town of Cambridge."

The operator simply said, "One moment, please."

While I waited, I said to Agatha, "Opavova—that's not a name you hear every day."

"Josef was Czechoslovakian."

"Should make the kids easier to track down."

The operator came back. "I'm afraid there are no listings for an Eva Opavova. I do have a number for Milo Opavova."

Milo was next down on my list. Had to be Martha and Josef's second-born. "Great," I said. "That's perfect."

The operator offered to connect me, but instead I asked for his number. That way if I didn't get through the first time I'd be able to call back.

Agatha grumbled as I punched in a 1, then the area code, then seven more digits. She acted like this call was costing her thousands of dollars, like every minute of phone time was torture.

A woman picked up and I asked, "Is this the residence of Milo Opavova?"

"We're not interested," the woman said and slammed down the phone.

My stunned reaction seemed to amuse Agatha, who grinned ear to ear.

I tried again. "Don't hang up! I'm not a telemarketer!"

There was silence on the other end, and then a somewhat embarrassed, "Oh."

"My name's Chris," I said, going for total transparency. "I'm here with a woman named Agatha Vanderjadt. She was a dear friend of Milo's parents."

"Milo's parents have been dead for years," the woman replied. She sounded like she wasn't totally sure if she wanted to trust me.

"I know," I told her. "And I'm sorry for your loss. Here's the thing: we're trying to locate some photos that might be in his possession."

"Why?"

Good question. I wasn't totally sure how to answer it. I couldn't very well say, "We suspect your husband of blackmailing old ladies."

When I didn't respond fast enough, the woman asked, "Are they worth money, these photos?"

I didn't know how to answer that question either, so I said, "I'd feel more comfortable discussing this matter with your husband, if you don't mind."

"My husband?" the woman spat. "What's he got to do with this?"

Now I was really confused. "Aren't you Milo Opavova's wife?"

"No," she said. "I'm his daughter."

"Oh." I guess wasn't expecting the man to have adult children. "Well, I'd still like to talk with Milo, if that's okay."

There was a strange sort of silence on the line, and then a bit of a choking sound. It wasn't until the woman spoke again that I realized she was crying. "I'm afraid my father can't talk to you right now." Her voice was stilted, stoic, and yet filled with an undercurrent of emotion. "He can't talk to anyone right now. He had a stroke and—"

Milo's daughter erupted into sobs that, quite frankly, ripped my heart to shreds. I wished I could reach through the phone lines and hold her... although I'm not sure what her husband would say about that. I've learned the hard way that most husbands don't take kindly to well-meaning men comforting their wives.

"Look, I'm really sorry," I said. "I didn't mean to stir things up."

"I practically live here these days," the daughter whispered into the phone. "My mom can't take care of him on her own. There's a personal support worker who comes in three hours a week, but do you know how many hours that leaves when we're the ones caring for him?"

"I'm really sorry."

"I never thought of my dad as an old man until now. I mean, he isn't even old. Fifty-seven! That's not old. He was always so strong, and now he's weak as a kitten."

This woman could use a good therapy session. Any other day I'd have listened as long as she wanted to talk, stranger or not. But Agatha was sitting across the kitchen table glaring at the wall clock, then glaring at me. I had to get off the phone.

"I'm sorry to interrupt," I said, "but I really need to track down what happened to these pictures. Is there anyone else in the family who might know?"

Sniffling, the woman said, "My Auntie Eva, probably. She was here a couple weeks ago, but now she's back home."

"Eva Opavova?"

"Eva Barbosa now. She took her husband's name. I didn't. But that was a different time, I guess."

Milo's daughter gave me her aunt's phone number and I wished her family well, then hung up and told Agatha what I'd learned.

"Little Milo had a stroke?" she said, shaking her head.

"He's not so little anymore. Fifty-seven, his daughter said."

"His *daughter*... Martha's *granddaughter*. Goodness. I remember when that baby was born, and now he's got children of his own."

"Adult children," I added. "Married and grown. Maybe with kids of their own. I didn't ask."

"Now you're just trying to make me feel old," Agatha said, swatting me across the table.

"Anyway, I got a number for the daughter, Eva. I'll call her now."

"All right," Agatha said dubiously. "But watch the clock this time."

"Okay, okay. Don't get your panties in a bunch." I glanced at the clock and did a double take when I realized it was almost eight at night. Pretty sure Agatha was usually in bed by this hour, and after working a double shift at the kennel I was about ready to crash. "On second thought, maybe we should pick this up in the morning."

Agatha's voice was surprisingly pleading when she said, "No! Do it now!"

How could I argue? I dialled the number and Eva herself picked up. Couldn't have been easier.

I introduced myself, same way I'd done with Milo's daughter, and she asked, with great excitement, "Miss Vanderjadt's there with you? Can you put her on speakerphone?"

I searched the handset for the right button, then said, "Sure."

"Am I on?" Eva asked. "Can you hear me?"

Agatha replied, "I can hear you just fine, so quit your hollering."

I glared at Agatha across the table. Best not to get on someone's bad side and then ask them for help.

But Eva seemed immune to Agatha's nastiness. She said, "I remember you from when I was just a little girl. You're one of my earliest memories!"

Agatha seemed a little frightened to hear that. "What kind of memory are we talking, here?"

"You took me for a pony ride."

"I did?"

"Yes," Eva said, with a glorious peal of youthful laughter. "There was some sort of circus... carnival... something like that. A touring show. My parents said there was more to it than just ponies, but all I remember is you fretting over the frilly little dress my parents put me in."

"Was I?" Agatha asked.

"Yes! You don't remember this? You were so worried I'd get muddy. I didn't care, of course. I was delighted to get on a pony."

Agatha shrugged at me across the table.

"I even have a picture," Eva added. "Me on a pony. It's one of my favourite photographs."

"Funny you should mention photographs," I cut in. "Because it just so happens that's what we're calling about."

"Oh, I've got tons! Let me grab them."

It sounded like Eva set down the phone and left the room, so I took the opportunity to say to Agatha: "Did you hear the tone of her voice?"

"What about it?" Agatha asked with her usual degree of surliness.

I took a deep breath to keep from joining in. Then I said, "You're not all happy-go-lucky like that when you're talking about porn shots of your mom and her lesbian lover."

"Keep your voice down," Agatha hissed across the table.

"Exactly!" I shot back. "That's exactly how you'd say it. You'd say, *Goodness yes, I did find some photographs.* And you don't offer to grab them!"

Over the speakerphone, I could hear Eva coming back into the room, so I shut my mouth. "I wish I could show these to you in person, Miss Vanderjadt. Wouldn't that be a walk down memory lane? Do you still live in Hillsgrave?"

"I do," Agatha replied. "And you're in Cambridge?"

"No, no," Eva said. "I'm living out west now. My brother still lives in Cambridge—in my parents' old house, in fact. He moved in with Father after Mother died. Gave everyone the impression he was doing it give Father a hand, but Milo's perpetually down on his luck. I'm sure that's why Father left him the house and the vast majority of the estate. Not that I'm bitter or anything."

I nodded along, not that the woman could see me over the phone.

"Anyway, the one thing Father specified should come specifically to me was his photography. He'd created quite a body of work over the course of his lifetime."

"Body of work?" Agatha mouthed across the table.

"And he left it all to you?" I asked Eva, to keep the conversation going.

"Yes, well, I'm a photographer by trade. Father was an amateur, but it was him that instilled in me the love of photography. Of course, when I got to school I found out everything he'd taught me was utterly wrong, but habits can be unlearned. What's important is the joy he planted in my heart..."

Agatha turned one hand into a puppet, mouthing *yammer-yammer-yammer* while Eva talked in detail about her craft.

It took a couple attempts before I managed to successfully interrupt.

"So Eva," I said. "Tell me about your father's pictures."

"Oh, there are boxes and boxes! He had his own dark room, you know, up in the attic of the Cambridge house."

"Interesting," I said, covering my mouth with one hand to stifle a yawn. "What did he like taking pictures of? Landscapes? Still life?"

"Heavens no," Eva laughed. "People! Always people! So many pictures of myself and my brother. Innumerable photos of my mother—some rather racy, to tell you the truth."

Agatha raised an eyebrow. I did the same.

How to put this across in a manner that didn't sound too crass? I asked, "Anybody else?"

"Oh sure," she said easily. "Lots of people-watching shots from Mother and Father's Paris trip."

That wasn't exactly what I meant.

"Any pictures of... *friends*?"

"Yes, of course. My parents hosted innumerable barbeques in our backyard. Plenty of photos taken there."

I looked to Agatha, feeling exhausted. I couldn't figure out how to get my question across clearly.

But Agatha could. She came right out and asked, "Any nudes?"

Eva offered an easy chuckle. "Yes, of course! Photographers adore the human form. I certainly do. In fact, nudes are my specialty. Sounds strange to say so, but I think it runs in the family. Father's favourite subject was Mother."

"Anyone else?" Agatha pried.

"Not that I've come across." Eva replied so immediately and with such guilelessness I found it hard to imagine she might be lying.

"You must come and see me if you're ever out west," Eva went on. "Any friend of my parents' is a friend of mine."

"I'm not keen on travel." Grabbing the phone off the table, Agatha hit the speakerphone button and hung up on poor Eva.

"Agatha!" I said. "You didn't even say goodbye. Or thank you! Bad enough you're rude to me, but when we're trying to extract information from people, you need to spread a little of that milk of human kindness."

"We were done with her," Agatha reasoned. "Anyway, she didn't give us much to go on. Either she lied and she does have those photos and she's the one trying to extract money from me, or she was telling the truth and she's got nothing to do with the blackmail."

"She didn't sound like she was lying," I said, blocking another yawn with the back of my hand. "She answered every question as soon as we asked it. People usually have to think a bit before they lie."

Getting up from the table, Agatha asked, "What are you yawning about? I thought you young queers liked to rock and roll all night."

"And party e-ve-ry day," I added, stifling yet another yawn. "But this young queer started work at 5 A.M. It's been a long day."

"I'll make a pot of tea," she said, hobbling toward the kettle.

Rising from the table, I started sleepwalking after her. "You sit down. I'll make the tea."

"No, *you* sit down," she growled. "*I'll* make the tea."

In all the time I'd been visiting Agatha, she'd never offered me a cup of tea, or anything else for that matter. I did so much for her and she seemed to expect it, even take it for granted, which could be infuriating at times. It's not like we were related or anything. But, in my mind, we were part of a larger family.

Anyway, I was raised to respect my elders... even when they acted like no-good brats.

I was too tired to argue with Agatha about who should make the tea. She told me to take a seat on the couch while the water boiled, but once my butt hit that well-worn cushion groove, I couldn't resist getting horizontal.

As I drifted off to Sandland, the last thing I could recall was Agatha's voice hollering, "Those muddy boots better not be soiling my sofa!"

Chapter Two

I woke up feeling like I'd spent the night under a bridge. Agatha's couch didn't have half the back support I needed after a long day's work, but on the plus side she'd apparently covered me with a blanket as I slept.

And taken off my boots.

Sunlight streamed in through the bay window. When I sat up, I could see the river sparkling like a diamond. A perfect spring day.

I got up to take a whiz and when I got back, I found Agatha in the kitchen. The Saturday paper was spread across her small table, with its corners hanging over the edges.

"Are you trying to read every section at once?" I asked.

Without looking up, she said, "There's tea in the pot."

"No coffee?"

"What do I look like, Alice's Restaurant?"

"Not even close." I smirked since she wasn't looking anyway, then said, "Sorry for sleeping on your couch. I didn't realize how tired I was."

She waved a hand dismissively.

"Have you eaten anything, Agatha?"

"There's eggs in the fridge," she said, flipping to the real estate insert. "It's criminal what houses go for these days. You know what I paid for this place?"

"Seven dollars and a goat."

She mumbled something unflattering as I got out the carton of eggs.

"You never answered my question: have you eaten breakfast?"

"I like my eggs poached," she replied.

Grabbing the milk, I told her, "You're getting scrambled."

"Tyrant."

In no time I had eggs going in the pan, plus slices of bread in the toaster. It didn't take much to get a good meal in your belly. Sometimes I wondered if Agatha was *trying* to wither away. Wouldn't surprise me in the least.

When breakfast was ready, I said, "Could you clear a place for these plates?"

Agatha didn't answer, but I got the sense she wasn't ignoring me deliberately this time. She seemed engrossed in real estate.

I put our plates on the travel section and asked, "What's so interesting?"

She pointed to a picture of a quaint older home and said, "This is where they lived. This was their house."

"Whose house?" I asked, biting into a piece of toast.

The crunch attracted Agatha's attention. "You've got toast? Where'd you get toast?"

"I made you a slice too," I said, pushing her plate closer.

She grabbed it greedily, like a child.

But she still hadn't answered my question, so I asked it again: "Whose house, Agatha?"

"Well, who've we been talking about all this time?" she sneered, like I'd asked the world's stupidest question.

Shaking my head, I said, "I don't know who *you've* been talking about. I just woke up."

"Last night," she said. "Last night! Your memory can't be that bad, unless you've fried it with drugs. Your generation! Smoking this and snorting that. Now it's prescription pills. You steal them from old people. Is that why you're always here quote-unquote *helping* me? To pinch my pills?"

"Agatha!" Honestly, after everything I'd done for the old broad I didn't know whether to laugh or cry. "Where is this coming from?"

"I just read an article about it," she said, shuffling the paper. "Says you young people steal pills and pop 'em at school."

I couldn't help chuckling. "At school, Agatha? I'm thirty-five years old."

"Maybe you sell 'em on the streets."

I let my head collapse in my hands. So she thought I was a drug dealer on the mean streets of Hillsgrave, did she? "Agatha, you need to stop reading the big city paper. Just stick to the Hillsgrave Howler from now on, okay?"

"They only print the Howler on Wednesdays. What am I supposed to read the rest of the week?"

"I don't know. A book, maybe?"

I picked up my fork and shovelled eggs into my face as fast as I could. I'd had about as much Agatha as I could handle for one day. Maybe I'd drop in at the kennel and take a few of my favourite pups for a hike. With weather like this, nothing could beat walking a dog.

Agatha scooped scrambled eggs onto her fork and tentatively inserted them into her mouth. Instantly, she made a face. "Hand me that salt and pepper, will you?"

Growling, I reached across the counter and smacked the salt and pepper shakers down in front of her.

"Watch the paper!" she cried, brushing bits of pepper off the house she'd drawn my attention to before calling me a drug dealer. "That was their house, you know—Martha and Josef. You talked to their daughter last night. This is the house they lived in before they moved to Cambridge."

It was all coming together now. Agatha's nonsense finally made sense in my mind. "Martha and Josef's old house is up for sale?"

"Open house today and tomorrow, noon until two."

"And it's right here in town?"

She nodded. "Sandhurst Circle."

"We should go," I said without hesitation. "Sandhurst Circle is right around the corner—walking distance from here!"

A strange expression came over Agatha. I would have called it fear if I thought her capable of such an emotion. In fact, she seemed terrified.

But why?

"You don't want to go?" I asked.

Her expression was hard to read.

"I'll tell you why I think we should," I went on, counting off reasons on my fingers. "We talked to Martha and Josef's kids and we hit a brick wall. If those blackmail photos weren't with the ones their daughter has in her possession, they must not have been at the Cambridge house. And don't you think it's a little suspicious that their old Hillsgrave house goes on the market and you get this blackmail notice at exactly the same time?"

"You think the photographs were left at the house here in town when Martha and Josef moved to Cambridge?"

"They're pretty risqué photos, Agatha. I mean, maybe not so much today, but at the time couldn't Joseph have been arrested for shooting them? Couldn't you and Martha have been arrested for appearing in them?"

"We could have been jailed, photos or no photos. Just for doing what we did behind closed doors. You can't imagine the secrecy."

She was right. I couldn't. Sure I wasn't as young as Agatha pegged me for, but I wasn't old enough to remember a time when love was illegal.

"Maybe they stashed the photographs somewhere discreet," Agatha went on. "Under floorboards, behind a false wall..."

"They wouldn't have wanted little Eva to come across that sort of thing."

"Right, exactly."

Agatha seemed hurt. "It's a shame to think they didn't care enough to bring those photos along to Cambridge."

Weird to see Agatha wearing her aching heart on her sleeve.

"Moving house is hectic," I said. "I'm sure it was just an oversight."

She grunted in a non-committal way.

"So we'll check the place out," I said. "What time is it? Oh, still early. Give me an hour to run home and shower, then we'll walk over for the open house."

Agatha shook her head. "You go on your own. I'm not too curious."

I couldn't believe her. "Someone's blackmailing you and you don't care enough to figure out who?"

"I bet it was Milo. You heard what his sister said: always down on his luck, lived with his father for years. I bet he found those photos and figured he could make a quick buck."

"But Milo had a stroke. His daughter gave me the impression that he's pretty much out of commission."

"So maybe he sent the letter months ago and it got tied up in the post. Or maybe his daughter sent it. The apple doesn't fall far from the tree."

"Agatha," I moaned. "What are the chances? It's far more likely this blackmail is tied to the place that just came on the market. Now do you want to go to the open house or not?"

She crossed her arms over her chest like a petulant child.

"Fine," I said. "I'll go myself."

"Fine," she said. "You do that."

I stormed toward the door, but when I got there I realized I was only wearing socks on my feet. "What did you do with my boots, Agatha?"

"Are you blind? They're right there by the front door!"

"Where?" I shouted.

"Right there!"

I couldn't see them anywhere. "Come and show me."

She hesitated for a long moment before bleating, "No."

As I walked up the stairs between the front door and the main level of Agatha's house, it dawned on me why she wouldn't come along. Gently, I asked, "Agatha, when was the last time you left your house?"

From the top of the stairs, I could see straight through to the kitchen. She wouldn't meet my gaze, and she didn't answer my question.

"You can't get down these stairs, can you?"

"Nosy Parker."

"Agatha, answer the question!"

"What's it to you?" she sneered.

I couldn't believe this woman sometimes. "What's it to *me*? I *care* about you, that's what! God knows why, but your wellbeing *matters* to me."

"No it doesn't."

"Oh, that's right. I forgot, I'm just here to steal your pills."

I looked for my boots again and spotted them at the bottom of the second set of stairs going down to the basement. Agatha must have tossed them down the first flight and they bounced off the front door, then tumbled down the basement set. I shoved my feet in them, feeling angry with Agatha and also ashamed of myself for yelling at her.

Stomping back up to the main level, I asked, "What if I carried you?"

"I'm not an invalid!"

"I know you're not, but you obviously need some help coming and going, so I'm offering. For Christ's sake, Agatha, you are infuriating!"

She got up from the table. I don't know why I'd never noticed this before, but she always kept at least one hand on the walls and appliances and countertops as she made her way across the kitchen. Maybe because her personality was so forceful, I hadn't realized she was so unsteady on her feet.

When she got to the junk drawer, she pulled out a flyer from a store that carried wheelchairs and walkers and an assortment of accessibility technologies. Without saying a word, she left the room.

"Want me to—"

She interrupted me quickly, saying, "You stay there. Don't move an inch."

Agatha returned to the kitchen with a stack of cash poking out from the pocket of her bathrobe.

"I want that one," she said, pointing to one of the walkers featured in the ad. "If you hold the front end it'll get me down those stairs all right. And then I can go to the open house."

Suddenly there weren't enough hours in the day. "Agatha, this store is an hour's drive from here."

"Well, you'd better get a move on, then." She handed me the stack of cash.

"Don't you think you should come along? To make sure it's the right size or... I don't know... shape?"

"Takes me a while to complete my ablutions," she said. "Don't dally. Open house is noon to two, remember."

How could I forget?

As I rushed home to shower and change my clothes, I couldn't help feeling like a dolt for not noticing Agatha's mobility problems. They seemed so obvious, in retrospect. What she really needed was one of those chairlift contraptions that let you ride up your stairs instead of walking. That way she could come and go as she pleased, without having to rely on me or anyone else.

Could it be that I was her only visitor?

The only other human she ever talked about was the teenager who delivered her groceries. Delivery wasn't actually a service the local market offered, but Agatha could be pretty convincing. If she called up your business and told you to bring her a carton of eggs and three bananas, you damn well brought her a carton of eggs and three bananas.

I also couldn't help wondering how much money she had in the house, and where exactly it was stored. I'd never come across stacks of cash, but I hadn't exactly been looking.

Could it be that she had enough dough under her mattress to pay off the blackmailer?

And, if she did, who would know that? I came to her house three times a week and I didn't know.

Before heading out of town to buy Agatha's walker, I had to satisfy my own curiosity. I stopped in at the local market full of Saturday morning shoppers and cornered the kid stocking shelves.

"You deliver groceries to Agatha Vanderjadt, right?"

The pimple-faced kid seemed intimidated by me—or maybe just put off by the smell of dog I could never get out of my clothes. He said, "Miss Vanderjagt calls almost every day. I get here for my shift after school and my boss hands me a bag. First thing I do is take it over on my bike."

"And she pays you money?"

"She doesn't tip me, if that's what you mean."

I smirked. "No, I wouldn't expect her to tip you or anybody else. But how does she pay for her groceries? Is it on account? On a credit card? By cheque?"

"No, she pays cash—has exact change laid out on the kitchen table every time."

"Where does the money come from?"

He shrugged. "How should I know?"

"Does she ever invite you in?"

"Invite me? No, I just walk in. I have to bring the food into the kitchen because she can't get down those stairs."

The kid who delivered her groceries knew this and I didn't?

"I don't hang around for a tea party, if that's what you mean. Old ladies creep me out, and her house smells like pee. I don't think she flushes for number one."

That much was true, but the kid didn't have to call attention to it.

I wasn't sure what else to ask, so I just thanked the teen and left.

As I drove out of town, I replayed our conversation in my mind. He didn't seem to know or care much about Agatha, despite seeing her every day. But that's what I'd have been like at his age. Too much else on my mind to care about some housebound old lady.

It took even longer than anticipated to drive to the wheelchair place. Lucky I didn't run out of gas. And, speaking of luck, they had in stock the walker Agatha wanted. The saleswoman thought she could flirt her way into selling me a bunch of add-ons, and any other day that might have been true. But I was running out of time, so all I took from her was the sales receipt and a brochure for stair lifts.

In and out and back on the road. Still, it was past one o'clock when I got back to Agatha's.

"Took you long enough!" Agatha shouted as I tumbled through the door carrying the box with her walker inside. "The open house ends at two."

"I know, I know!"

She was sitting in the chair closest to the stairs, wearing a visor, a huge pair of sunglasses, a spring jacket, and holding her purse. She had on a pastel pink pair of pants, which was a surprise. It was true that she always wore skirts and dresses. Maybe she was worried about a long skirt getting caught in the wheels and the walker inadvertently pantsing her.

"What's that?" she asked, pointing at the giant cardboard box. "Where's my walker?"

"Your walker's in the box. I have to put it together."

"Well that's just perfect," she griped. As I hauled the box up the stairs, she asked, "Where's my change?"

Groaning, I set the box down in the living room and sliced it open with my pen knife. Putting it together took no time at all. Setting it at the right height for Agatha—now that was traumatic.

"It's still not right," she said when I moved the handlebars up a notch. "None of these settings are right."

"Well, this is why I said you should come along to buy it! You couldn't have tested it out in the store!"

"Put it down again. The last setting was better."

"You said it was too low!"

"But I was standing up straight. I want to see if it's comfortable while I'm walking."

I did what she asked without too much griping, and when she'd taken a brief walk around the living room she decided the setting was satisfactory.

All that was left was to hold the walker steady while she descended the staircase.

"Well, this is no good," she said as her walker tilted on a downward slope.

"It's not made for stairs, Agatha. What you really need is a stair lift. Remind me to give you the pamphlet I picked up."

"I'll remind you to hand over my change—that's what I'll remind you about."

"You think I'm trying to steal five dollars and seventy-three cents from you? What about the forty bucks' worth of gas I put in my van to get back into town?"

"Whine, whine, whine," she said as she stomped down the stairs. "You always were a complainer, even as a child."

"I could let go of this walker right now."

That shut her up.

We made it down the stairs and out the door without a single scrape or bruise.

I expected her to head to my van.

"Where are you going?" I asked as Agatha allowed her walker guide her toward the sidewalk.

"Like you said, it's just around the corner. And isn't it a beautiful day? A lovely day! Just lovely!"

She seemed pretty gleeful to be outside. Really made me wonder when she last left the house. So I didn't argue. I just followed along.

Something started squeaking as we made our way down the sidewalk, and I kept asking Agatha to stop so I could check that all the wing nuts were tight enough. But as we turned the corner onto Sandhurst Circle, I realized it wasn't the walker that was squeaking—it was *Agatha*.

"Jesus Murphy! Can't you control your farts?"

"Nope," she said simply—dare I say *proudly*?

"Just try to make a good impression when we get to the open house," I told her. "And for Christ's sake, don't yell at anybody!"

Agatha harrumphed as we approached the quaint little house that had been listed in the paper. There was a For Sale sign rammed into the front yard, which I zipped by so I could help Agatha turn onto the front walk.

"Give me a moment," she said distractedly as she stared up at the house.

I moved out of her way so she could see it better. I'd never been sure how much Agatha could see through those thick glasses and clouded eyes, but in that moment I suspected she was seeing the past. Memories seemed to fly across her field of vision, and I wished I could get inside her head. She'd obviously shared quite a bond with the couple who'd lived there long ago—with Martha, certainly.

"Let's go in," I said softly. "It's almost two."

Right on cue, the front door opened and a man in a slick blue suit emerged. His bald head and cylindrical face looked vaguely familiar. He must have been the real estate agent, because he was fitting a lock box on the door.

"Is the open house over?" I called. "Did we miss it?"

The man in the suit swivelled around and painted a phoney smile across his lips.

Then recognition sparked, and a different sort of phoney smile took over.

"Is that Miss Vanderjadt? As I live and dream!" Taking the front steps gingerly in his polished shoes, he said, "It is I: Damon O'Leary! Certainly you remember me from Hillsgrave Primary School."

Agatha fixed on him, bending forward, leaning so much of her weight on the walker that I had to grab it so it wouldn't fly forward. "Damon O'Leary? I do remember you. Little hellion, you were. Used to put earthworms in little girls' lunch pails."

The real estate agent offered an insecure titter. "Yes, well, that was so long ago. Water under the willows."

"We were hoping to see the house," I said. "Miss Venderjadt used to be friends with the owners."

"My parents?" the agent asked. "I didn't know that! Although, to be fair, once I left town to establish a successful career in the city's best real estate agency, I must admit I didn't visit as often as they would have liked. In fact, with all the million-dollar homes on my roster, I wouldn't normally take on a small bean like this one. But how could I say no to Dearest Mater?"

Who was this guy trying to impress? Probably Agatha. He hadn't so much as glanced in my direction.

Agatha was in fine form, and equally unimpressed. She said, "Slow down with the fast talk, Slick Willy. You're saying your parents are the sellers?"

"You got it," Damon O'Leary replied. "Now I know what you're thinking, Miss Vanderjadt: how did Ma and Pa O'Leary manage to raise five rambunctious boys in a house this size? Well, in point of truth, this isn't the house I grew up in. My parents bought this haven of tranquility as empty nest-eggs. It was their downsizing home. Now, bless their hearts, the house has become too much to maintain. They've decided to move into Oak Harbour, the retirement home down the river. Beautiful facility. Really top-notch."

Agatha shot me a look that required no interpretation. No self-respecting elderly person *decided* to move into Oak Harbour. That was a decision their kids made on their behalf.

"How are your brothers doing?" Agatha asked.

"Good, good, good," Damon O'Leary said, rubbing his hands together. They made an unappealing dry skin sound, like rubbing two blocks of wood one against the other. "My brothers are spread all across the country these days, in various modes of employ. Not a-one of them is as successful as me, I might add."

"The middle child always has something to prove," Agatha muttered.

Cupping his hand behind his ear, the real estate agent leaned forward. "Squeeze me? Baking powder?"

I nearly groaned, but reminded myself that I'd advised Agatha to be on her best behaviour. I could offer myself the same piece of advice.

"Can we see the house?" I asked. "It isn't two o'clock yet."

"Sure, sure! I thought I might sneak off early, but you caught me, you lucky loons!" Damon O'Leary took a step back and considered Agatha's walker. "You might have trouble getting that doohicky up these front steps."

Agatha told the man, "I can walk up steps, so long as I've got a railing and this strapping young fellow to help me."

I went from feeling invisible to feeling indispensable in less than a second. More than that, hearing Agatha refer to me as a *strapping young fellow*... well, stuff like that never got old. I should be over it by now, but perceptions that fit the way I felt still pleased me to no end. Being seen as strong. Being seen as a man, plain and simple.

Damon O'Leary yanked Agatha's walker out of her way, shoved it in the house, and held the door open for us to enter. His beady eyes were all over me, at once slimy and blazing, as he asked, "Did we go to school together?"

"I don't think so."

Agatha couldn't leave well enough alone. While I helped her up those three front steps, she said, "Well, in fact, you boys did go to the same school but not quite at the same time. Damon would have been in the older grades while you were still quite young, Chris."

"Chris," Damon reflected. "You *do* look familiar. Do you have a sister?"

"Yup," I said before Agatha could cut it.

"Right, right, that's what I'm remembering: she was just a wee young thing, but she insisted on playing ball with the older boys. Spunky little gal, that sister of yours."

"I'll be sure to let her know."

I gripped Agatha's arm a little too tight as I led her up those stairs, hoping and praying she'd keep her mouth shut. Successfully sleazy real estate agent Damon O'Leary didn't need to know the spunky little gal playing ball with the older boys had been me.

That fake sister of mine, I tell you, she got up to some hijinks in her day.

When we'd landed ourselves inside the house and Agatha was back behind the wheels of her rolling walker, Damon O'Leary handed me a piece of paper with a picture of the house and a bunch of numbers. "Here, I'll give you the spec sheet. Only two bedrooms and no stairs in the interior, so perfect for the older population. You could put a ramp out front and bibbity-doo-daa-day! Accessible entrance!"

I worried that Agatha would say she wasn't looking to buy this house, but she was in as much of a daze now as she'd been outside. "Everything's changed," she said softly.

"That's right!" the agent replied. "I had the place renovated top to basement before putting it on the market."

I thought about those pictures of Agatha, where Martha and Josef might have stashed them, and I asked, "The attic too?"

"The whole shebang! My parents, God love 'em, they weren't able to keep up maintenance in the last couple years. Money gets tight toward the end."

I glanced at Agatha, but she'd waddled into a kitchen like you wouldn't believe: granite countertops, all new flooring and cupboards. It was like a dream, to me, but I could sense that Agatha wanted to rediscover her personal history in this house, and it was nowhere to be found.

"The roof leaked," Damon O'Leary went on, "so of course I had a new one put on, and in the process my contractor discovered some rot in the attic beams. I insisted they be replaced. That led to her pulling out all the old fiberglass insulation and replacing it with—"

"Your contractor... is a *woman*?"

I guess I must have bristled visibly, because the real estate agent said, "Yes, but don't worry—the work is tip-top." He pulled a business card from his pocket and, in a titillated stage-whisper, said, "Maxine Holdstern, General Contractor... and lady-lover to boot! I must admit, I tested her mettle in the latter regard."

Poor Max. I tried not to shudder too hard at the thought of this sleazeball hitting on her. Just the sight of her business card made me morose. I didn't want to show my hand too much in front of Damon O'Leary, so I pocketed the card and followed Agatha into the kitchen.

Of course, by the time I'd entered the kitchen she was no longer there. Must have turned the corner into the dining room.

"As you can see, we went with laminate flooring." I guess he was trying to sell this house to me now. "Looks just like hardwood, but holds up much better, especially in the kitchen."

"Yeah, it's great," I said without really looking.

But then I actually did look at it and wow, yeah, it looked great. Max did amazing work. I could see a lot of her taste in this kitchen, and it made me too sad for words.

"I must apologize for the rank odour in here," the agent went on, waving his hand in front of his nose. "I can assure you this kitchen doesn't normally smell like wet dog."

"That's probably me." I smelled my shirt, and I wasn't all that subtle about it. "I work in a kennel five days a week. Can't get that smell out of my van. Or my clothes."

"What a relief," Damon O'Leary said with what struck me as almost-genuine laughter. "I was beginning to think maybe it was me. I have three darling Yorkies at home, though I don't tend to allow them anywhere near my office attire."

"Don't worry," I said. "You're in the clear."

Damon O'Leary fiddled with his pen as I pressed my palm against the cool countertop. "So, Chris, you're some kind of POW for Miss Vanderjadt?"

"Heh. Something like that."

"And your position is... live-in?"

"Not yet," I said.

"Well, if you were to move in here, there's certainly room enough for yourself and Miss Vanderjadt. Why don't we look at the bedrooms?"

"The attic space," I pressed. "Is it big enough that I could build myself a room up there?"

"Unfortunately not," Damon said, with an excessive pout. "It's really more of a crawl space up there, perfect for stashing away a few boxes. Nowhere near enough space for a strapping lad to stand."

Had Martha and Josef stashed a few boxes of photos up there? And then forgotten about them?

Might as well ask the agent. What's the worst that could happen?

But I wasn't totally sure how to broach the subject.

"Your parents lived here," I said. "And Agatha's friends before that."

"Ahh, the Rosettis," he replied. "Fine family."

"No, her friends were Martha and Josef Opavova. They had a daughter and then a son, and then they moved. But this was years ago."

Damon O'Leary nodded knowingly. "This darling home has changed hands innumerable times over the years. It's a perfect starter home for a young couple. Room for the newlyweds, room for a nursery. But as soon as that second baby comes along, well, suddenly the house starts to feel a little cramped."

So the house had seen many owners since Martha and Josef. Great. That didn't exactly help in our effort to track down the blackmailer.

I had to ask a more direct question and hope this guy wouldn't clue in as to why. "With all those different families moving through this house, I bet you found a lot of treasures up in the attic."

He twitched, then ran his hand down his pink and yellow striped tie. "You'd have to ask my contractor about those matters. Her people handled the house-clearing, demolition, all that."

Max handled the house-clearing? When the house had belonged to the real estate agent's own parents? That seemed a little impersonal. But I guess that was Damon O'Leary's style. Everything was surface with this guy. He acted like he cared, but only long enough to sell you something.

"I'd better find Agatha," I told him, and wandered into the dining room.

Boy, did Max do a great job with this place. Not that I knew what it looked like before, but the finished product was truly excellent. Part of me was irked by the fact that she was doing so well for herself, running her own business when I was still cleaning up dog crap for a living, but another more generous part of me was actually kind of happy for her.

When I'd moved through the TV room and still not found Agatha, I turned the corner into a narrow hallway. My first thought was *no way Agatha's walker would fit down here*, but sure enough there she was at the end of the hall, standing in the entryway to one of the bedrooms.

I rushed ahead, but Damon kept up, hot on my heels as I looked over Agatha's shoulder.

"This is it," I said. The room in the photographs. Much about it had changed, but I recognized the chunky wooden border around the window.

Damon O'Leary came up behind me, asking, "Would you like to put in an offer?"

"We'll have to think about it," I told him.

"I understand," he replied. "There's a lot to talk about. My direct number is on the spec sheet, if you should have any questions after you leave."

Agatha remained strangely silent as she gazed across the room.

So I said, "We'll be sure to give you a call if we do. Come on now, Agatha. Let's get going. You haven't had any lunch."

When she didn't budge, Damon chuckled victoriously. "In her mind, she's moved in already!"

I forced a laugh. "Come on, Agatha. It's past two. You must be starving."

I'd never seen her so lost. Obviously the past she'd enjoyed in this room was far preferable to the present day.

I said her name one more time, and finally she turned to me. I could see in her eyes that she was reconciling past with present.

She nodded. "Let's go."

Damon O'Leary talked at us while we made our way through the house. He offered Agatha help down the stairs, but she said, "Chris can handle it. He's solid muscle, you know."

That was far from true, but nice to hear.

The real estate agent hovered in the doorway while I held the walker and Agatha stepped down—one foot, then the other, slow as you please.

I didn't say anything until the house was out of sight, because I felt Damon O'Leary's beady eyes burning into my back. I didn't want him hearing our conversation.

"That was the room from the pictures," I said once we'd turned off Sandhurst Circle.

Agatha didn't reply. She seemed content to walk in silence.

When we arrived at her house, she asked me to open the gate. There was a flat path to her backyard, which boasted a patio table and chairs that looked as though they hadn't been used in the better part of a decade.

"It's such a lovely day," she said, sitting on the part of her walker that doubled as a seat. "I'd like to spend some time out here while you get lunch going."

I'd only mentioned lunch to get us out of the open house. I didn't think she'd expect me to make it for her. But it's not like I could say no. Anyway, Agatha seemed so forlorn after viewing that bedroom. She obviously needed some time to herself.

As I entered through the kitchen door, Agatha called out, "Could you bring me the little radio on the sideboard? And the photocopies..."

Seemed strange that she'd want to look at them outside, but with her high fences and tree-bound property it's not like the neighbours would see. So I brought her the things she wanted and went about fixing us each a tuna-fish sandwich with a side of five-bean salad—my mother's recipe. The only dish I remember ever helping her with when I was young. She often tried to get me baking, but my brother Robbie would come along and want to help, and she'd say to him: "No, Robbie. Baking is just for girls, not for boys."

After that, of course, I never wanted to help my mother bake. Baking wasn't for boys. Why couldn't she see I was a boy like Robbie? Why couldn't anybody see that?

The salad should have marinated overnight to let all that vinegar seep into the beans. I let it sit while I ran a broom across the creaking hardwood and a mop across the kitchen floor. For someone who couldn't get around too easily, Agatha kept her house neat and tidy. She just needed a hand with this and that. And I didn't mind lending a hand. Don't ask me why. Agatha didn't exactly express much gratitude about it.

When I stepped out the kitchen door to serve Agatha her lunch, she wasn't at the patio table where I'd left her. Neither were the radio or the photocopies. Christ, don't tell me the blackmailer got tired of waiting and decided to kidnap her instead!

Or maybe she'd decided, with her newfound freedom, she'd walk on down to the bank and take out the money in question.

No, impossible. The bank was too far to walk, and anyway it was only open nine to noon on Saturdays.

Before I could dream up any more danger scenarios, the smoky scent of fire hit my nose.

Dear God, what now?

Chapter Three

I followed my nose around the back of the house, finding Agatha on the ground beside a rusted-out fire pit.

"Agatha! What happened? Did you fall?"

"No, I most certainly did not fall," she said gruffly. "That said, I can't quite get up on my own, so you might as well give me a hand now you're here."

"What are you burning?" I asked as flames licked the cooking grate. "Is that leaves in there?"

"Papers," she told me.

I glanced around as I helped Agatha up onto the walker's seat. The radio was down in the grass, tuned to a station that played lots of Sinatra and Dean Martin. Beside the radio was a barbeque lighter. The blackmail photocopies were nowhere to be found.

"Agatha," I said. "Did you burn the photos?"

Haughtily, she replied, "No, I burned the *copies*."

"Why would you do that?"

She waved dismissively. "I don't need those things lying around. What happens when I die? They'll only be found by whoever clears out the house."

Part of me wanted to ask *What do you care? You'll be dead*, but instead I grabbed the hose and said, "Let's put out this fire before you wind up burning the place down."

She didn't object. She'd burned what she'd set out to burn, but she obviously knew I'd object or why do it in secret?

"I thought you said you were making lunch," Agatha said in a huff.

I wrapped the hose back around its cradle and turned off the water. I couldn't accomplish one thing before she was on to the next.

I said, "Lunch is ready. It's at the patio table. I thought we could eat outside, seeing as it's so nice out."

"Actually, it's a little chilly for my taste."

Half an hour ago it was a lovely day! God, Agatha! Sometimes that woman made me crazy.

"Fine," I said. "We'll eat inside."

"No, no, no. Don't go to any trouble. We'll eat out here if that's what you want."

"It's not about what *I* want," I growled. "You said..."

I had to stop myself. It just wasn't worth getting into a war of words with the woman.

Agatha grimaced at the tuna-fish and said the bean salad was a little sweet for her taste, but she ate everything I'd served her and then asked for more, so I guess that says something.

"That real estate agent, Damon O'Leary," I said. "You taught him in school."

Agatha nodded. "Some kids are no good but they grow out of it. Other kids are no good and they stay no good all their lives."

"I asked him if he came across any interesting stuff from former owners when they did all those renovations. He said I'd have to ask Max about that."

"Max who?"

"Maxine Holdstern, the contractor who redid the house. I thought maybe we'd give her a call, track her down after lunch, ask her a few questions."

Agatha sighed in a distinctly woe-is-me fashion. "Oh, I'm too tired for that. All this running around and I'm ready for my nap."

My stomach flip-flopped. On the one hand, I wanted Agatha by my side when I met up with Max for the first time since our big break-up. On the other hand, I didn't want Agatha embarrassing me—farting and so forth.

Maybe bean salad wasn't the best idea.

"Open the door," Agatha said with alarm. "I need to get inside. Now!"

She bolted up from her walker and teetered side to side as I held the door.

I was about to follow her when she said, "That salad's got me on the go-go-go!"

"Sorry," I shouted after her.

From down the hall, I heard her say, "Don't be! When you're my age, it's just what a body needs!"

That was really more than I needed to know, but Agatha didn't seem to mind oversharing.

While Agatha was in the bathroom, I grabbed one of her many cordless phones and dialled the number on Max's business card.

She picked up and said, "Miss Vanderjadt? From Hillsgrave Public School?"

"No, Max. It's me."

For a second, I thought the line had gone dead. And then I worried maybe Max didn't recognize my voice. True, it had grown deeper since we were together, but I had to believe she'd know the sound of my voice whether I talked like Minnie Mouse or James Earl Jones.

"The call display," she said. "It tripped me up."

"Sorry. I'm using Agatha's phone—Miss Vanderjadt's phone. I help her out with this and that, you know."

"Oh, I know," Max said meaningfully. "Animals and elders. I *know* you, Chris." Then she asked, "Where'd you get this number? This is my business line."

"Sorry," I said, feeling ridiculously flustered. "Should I hang up and call your home number?"

"No," she said, with a glittering laugh. "No, I'm not at home. I'm on a jobsite."

"Oh. Sorry. You're working. I can let you go."

She laughed again, and said, "The best thing about being my own boss is that I only answer to myself. And my clients. Actually, mostly my clients—90% clients, 10% me. But it's still better than working for the man."

"Sure, sure. Sounds great." I didn't know what to say. I was babbling, and she knew it because she kept laughing. "Sorry," I said. "It's just... it's good to hear your voice."

"Good to hear yours too. It sounds... you sound... *different*."

"Oh. Sorry."

"No! It's good. I like it. Soon you'll be singing Old Man River like nobody's business."

"I don't know about that," I said, but it was certainly nice to hear. "Look, Max, I had a reason for calling. I wanted to ask you about a project you worked on: a house on Sandhurst—"

"Wait a sec, Chris. My client wants a word about finishes." She growled and whispered into the phone: "I thought we settled this two weeks ago. Grrr!" And then she said, "Sorry, gotta go. How about we discuss your project over dinner. Meet at the usual haunt?"

"Yeah. Yeah, sounds great."

"Say seven?"

"I'll be there."

When I hung up, I had a smile on my face and a knot in my stomach. I tried to set aside the reasons we broke up. All those heart-shredding arguments seemed so distant now that we'd been apart for so long. I still loved her. That was the truth. I would always love her, no matter what.

And now we had a dinner date.

I didn't know what Agatha was talking about. There wasn't a chill in the air. In fact, as I sat in my patio chair and closed my eyes, the sun shone warm upon my face. This well and truly was a good day.

When I popped into the house to set the phone back in its cradle, Agatha was just emerging from her bedroom. She'd changed out of her pink pastel pants and into one of her around-the-house cotton dresses.

"Do you want me to put in a load before I head out?"

She nodded, seeming relieved that she didn't have to ask, much less admit to having pooped her pants. "The laundry basket's in the bathroom. I might have a soak after you leave."

"Okay," I said. "Just be careful. I don't want to get here tomorrow and find you drowned in your own bathtub."

I shouldn't say things like that. Might give her ideas.

But Agatha said, "I can't die yet. We've got a mystery to solve."

Chapter Four

I didn't see Max's truck in the lot when I got to the Italian place we'd frequented as a couple. I was too nervous to set foot in that restaurant alone, so I waited in the car, tapping my fingers against the wheel to the music in my mind.

Had I dressed up too much? Nice clean shirt—the blue one she'd bought me. Had a little shimmer to it, real dressy. Black trousers, a black tie. I knew the look she went for, and I didn't mind playing to her tastes. Especially since I knew, no matter how well I dressed, I'd still smell like dogs.

A shiny new truck pulled into the lot, and I knew instinctively Max was in it even though I couldn't see through the dark windows. The decal gave her away, a little logo with a hammer and nail, just like on her business card.

I started making up taglines for her business: *Get hammered with Maxine Haldstern.* Better yet, *Get nailed by Max!*

Christ, I was getting loopy with nerves. My legs were shaking as I stepped out of the van.

I walked toward her new truck as she hopped down from the cab. The things that woman could do in heels blew my mind. The one time my mom forced me into a pair, I managed to fall flat on my face in front of every graduate of Hillsgrave Public School—and their parents.

But Max was a different story. Max was a dream: the sleeveless black dress she wore showed off her tall, athletic build. The chestnut brown hair she usually tied back for work now danced across her bare shoulders. She grabbed a small purse and a royal blue wrap off the seat and then gave the door a good heave. I'd always been jealous of Max's muscles, but she worked for them... which was more than I could say for my own.

"You look... wow... just... wow!"

That's the best I could do.

She came over and wrapped one arm around me. I could smell her flowery perfume. I just hoped she couldn't smell dog.

"You look good too," she said, tentatively touching my face. I almost didn't shave, just so she'd see the stubble growing in, but then I wondered if I'd be leaving it just to prove something. So I did shave. I hope she liked the look. I think she did.

"I'm glad you dressed up," she said. "I wasn't sure if I should wear this or... but the weather, I mean it's so nice out today. Tomorrow it might snow, and then I'd be kicking myself for not taking advantage."

She was yammering and I was glad to hear it. Meant she was as nervous as I was.

"I'm really glad you called," she said. "Come on, let's go inside."

Stepping into that restaurant was like stepping back in time, to a time when me and Max were a couple and everything was easy.

Low lighting, dark wood, bruschetta. What more could you ask for?

"Look, I'm really sorry," she said, running her fingers up and down the stem of her wine glass. "Those things I said when we broke up... I was just plain *wrong*. I can't believe you're even speaking to me now. If *I* were you, I would never speak to me again."

"Water under the bridge," I said, because it was easier than talking about it.

"No, Chris." She cupped her hand over mine on the table. "All that stuff I said about you just wanting to transition to cash in on male privilege and enforce patriarchal hegemonies? That was really out of bounds."

I wished she hadn't repeated those words. I didn't want them to be fresh in my mind, even framed by an apology. "You don't have to say all this."

"Yes I do."

Our meals came: the mushroom risotto for her and the ossobuco for me. Max thanked our server with genuine gratitude, but waited for the young man to leave us alone before continuing her apology.

"I was so afraid of losing you," she said. "And not just losing *you*, but losing a part of *me* too. Coming out wasn't easy. I faced a lot of resistance."

"So did I," I assured her.

"But *you*, I mean you always *looked* like a lesbian. With you people were like *yeah, sure, that's a lesbian all right*. With me it was: *oh honey, you're just confused, it's a phase, you'll grow out of it*."

She'd told me all this before, but I could see what she was building toward this time.

"When you started thinking about transitioning, it made me feel like maybe all the naysayers were right. Because if you were a man, then we'd just be a run-of-the-mill straight couple and my mom could say *I told you so*."

"Max," I said, feeling a pleading sort of worry inside me. "You can't hang your entire identity on one relationship."

She nodded. We hadn't even touched our meals yet. She was still clinging to my hand as she said, "I know that now. My primary attraction is to women. Always has been. But I love you, and I think I always will, and I can't let myself worry what that implies or what other people think. None of that matters. Love is what matters."

I kissed her. Couldn't not. The sparkle in her eyes, the way the candle light made her skin glow, the sheer excitement in her voice... we were getting back together! My life was complete!

"Ahem."

When me and Max broke away from our kiss, the young server was standing by our table with a huge pepper grinder in his outstretched hands. "For you, Madame?"

I'm sure he had no clue why she burst out laughing, but she also managed to nod and point to her risotto.

The young man spritzed her dish with pepper shrapnel before turning to me. "And for you, Sir?"

Smiling widely, I said, "Please."

Chapter Five

It wasn't until our espressos and molten lava cakes arrived that Max said, "Oh! You wanted to consult with me on a project. Or was that just an excuse to get me out on a date?"

"It wasn't an excuse," I said, because I wanted her to know I was above trickery of any sort.

That's when I told her about Agatha Vanderjagt's blackmailer.

"So we went to the open house today and Damon O'Leary gave me your card."

Max shuddered. "Uck. I've worked for some misogynistic pinheads in this job, but that guy was just plain slithery."

I agreed 100% with her assessment of the real estate agent, but what I really wanted to know about were the pictures. "He said you had to redo a bunch of stuff in the attic."

"Oh yeah, I found plenty of interesting stuff stashed up there. I wish I'd known you were helping Miss Vanderjadt. Then I would have for-sure-for-sure returned all those photos and letters to her. To be honest, I thought she was long dead."

"Hold up," I said. "What photos and letters are we talking about?"

"Whole big boxes," Max replied as she dug into dessert. "An entire shoebox of love letters Agatha Vanderjadt had written to a woman named Martha. We figure the older generation doesn't know sex from a hole in the ground, but these women, Chris, they're our foremothers! You should have read some of this stuff. Talk about spicy!"

Despite all the time I spent with Agatha, I couldn't imagine her ever writing love letters. I guess she really was young once.

"And then the pictures!" Max went on. "Chris, my God, you should have seen them! You'd never have recognized Miss Vanderjadt."

I didn't bother reminding her that I had, in fact, seen the pictures—or at least photocopies. It was true that I wouldn't have recognized Agatha if she hadn't told me it was her. That's what led me to ask Max, "How did you know what you were looking at?"

"Mostly because of the letters," Max said. "I found those first. I'm not ashamed to say I spent an entire afternoon hunched in that musty attic, reading those love notes. It was bliss."

"And that's how you knew it was Agatha in the photos?"

Max shrugged. "It helped that photographs were labelled on the back: MO+AV. I put two and two together."

Whoever was blackmailing Agatha must have done the same: read the letters, connected the dots.

"Some of those pictures, Chris, I tell 'ya!" She fanned herself with the dessert menu. "I almost kept them for my own personal use."

"But you didn't keep them?" I asked, just to be sure.

"No, I donated all the pictures and letters to the local archives."

"Archives? Where, in town?"

Max laughed. "You didn't know we had archives, Chris? You've only lived in Hillsgrave your entire life."

"Yeah, but..."

"Did you ever go there for a field trip? I went. At least three times."

Field trips, yes, I remembered now. A crumbling whitewashed building on the main street. I'd been there too.

"If you want to know what happened to those photos, you'll have to ask Sonja Gorska."

"From school?"

"Yeah, she's been the town archivist ever since old Mrs. Lumpkin retired."

"Sonja Gorska," I said, picturing the girl I'd known at school, one year above me. "Does she still have that unibrow?"

Max laughed as she grabbed her purse. She stood from the table in an elegant sweeping motion. "I guess you'll have to pay her a visit to find out. Now, if you don't mind, I'm going to use the ladies' and then maybe you'd like to... drive me home?"

"But your truck is here," I said obliviously.

"True, but I've had a glass of wine."

"That was over an hour ago, and you've had an espresso since then. I'm sure you're fine to drive."

Max raised an eyebrow. "Maybe I want to get a ride from you."

When it finally dawned on me what she was asking for, I nearly passed out.

Chapter Six

When I arrived at Agatha's house, she called out to me from the kitchen: "Where have you been all day? It's nearly dinnertime!"

"It's eleven in the morning, Agatha, and do I need to remind you that I come here out of the goodness of my own heart? There's no court order compelling me to visit."

"Where were you last night?"

As I trudged up the front stairs, I felt kind of taken aback. Agatha wanted me to account for my whereabouts? Since when did I answer to her?

"I tried calling you at home," she said, pushing her empty tea cup across the table like I should take that as an instruction to refill it.

"Where'd you get my phone number?" I asked.

"You're in the book, genius."

Swiping her cup off the table, I said, "If you must know, I had a date."

"Well, whoop-dee-doo. A date! Aren't you just the king of the hill?"

"I'm not bragging, Agatha. You asked me where I was and I told you. Don't ask the question if you don't want to know the answer."

I set a fresh cup of tea in front of her, but she didn't touch it. "Aren't you curious why I was calling?"

"Looks like you're going to tell me either way."

She looked at me proudly and said, "I have a theory."

Groaning, I sat across from her at the table. "What's your theory?"

She leaned in excitedly, her eyes sparkling like a child's. "When you called Milo Opavova—that's Martha and Josef's son..."

"Yes, I know who Milo Opavova is."

"...well, remember his daughter said he couldn't come to the phone?"

"Right. Because he had a stroke."

Agatha raised a finger in the air, and then pointed it at me. "What if he didn't have a stroke?"

"But he did."

"We don't know that."

"His daughter said he did."

"Maybe she was lying. Maybe she's in on it."

"In on what?" I asked, really getting frustrated at this point.

"In on the blackmail! Maybe Milo isn't in Cambridge at all. Maybe he's here in town."

"Why would he be?"

"To pick up the money! Keep up, will you?"

Letting my head fall in my hands, I said, "Agatha, this is crazy."

"Easy for you to say. You're not the one being blackmailed."

"Look, I got some inside information about those pictures of you and Martha."

I expected Agatha to bark orders at me, or maybe just shout in some general way, but she simply sat across the table from me, waiting to hear what I had to say.

"We were right: Josef had stashed some pictures in the attic of their old house. And Martha stashed stuff too: the love letters you wrote her."

Agatha's brow furrowed. Her bottom lip hung open, and then, uncharacteristically, started to quiver. "They left all that behind?"

She was obviously heartbroken, but I couldn't not tell her. I tried to make it better, saying, "I'm sure they just misplaced that stuff, Agatha. You know how it is: the more you value something, the safer you try to keep it. You hide it somewhere nobody else will look, and then when you go to find it again..."

"How many pictures?" she asked. "How many letters?"

"A shoebox of letters. Even more pictures."

I watched Agatha touch her head gently, patting it here and there, like she was looking for a memory, like she could find it from the outside in.

And then she jerked, startled, and asked, "Who has them now? The pictures of me... the letters... do *you* have them?"

"No, Agatha, they were given to the town archives."

"Oh God," Agatha moaned. "Old Lady Lumpkin's seen naked pictures of me!"

It struck me as amusing that a woman as old as Agatha would refer to any other human as "Old Lady" Anything, but I thought I might bring her some comfort, saying, "Old Lady Lumpkin retired. Sonja Gorska's the archivist now."

"Sonja Gorska—I know that name."

"You must have taught her. She was one year above me at school."

"Unibrow," Agatha replied. "Tried hard, bless her heart, but she wasn't terribly clever, was she?"

"You tell me. You were her teacher."

"Who gave the photos to Sonja? How did she get them? Where did you find this out?"

"Slow down," I said, trying to get out of telling Agatha anything about Max or her involvement in all this. "One of the people working on the house remodel found the boxes of letters and photos."

"And he gave them to the archives? Why would he do that? Why not give them to me? Was he trying to embarrass me? Humiliate me? Who is he? Is he the blackmailer?"

"No, no, no Agatha. I think they just figured the pictures had historical relevance. I can tell you for sure this is someone who wants to see more gay and lesbian representation in all facets of life." Gee, one night with Max and I was already starting to talk like her. "They would have done this to advance queer representation."

Agatha swiped the air like she was face-slapping someone who wasn't there. "Oh, who gives a damn about representation? This is my *body* we're talking about! My *words*! My *life*! It belongs to no one but me."

I had trouble disagreeing with Agatha on that point. Would I want passages from my own personal journal passed among historians and interpreted as text? That was me on paper. Those pictures and letters—those were Agatha on paper.

"Let's go," I said.

"Go where?"

"See if the archives are open today."

Agatha smirked. "You're taking me on a field trip, eh?"

"Yeah," I said. "Ironic."

Chapter Seven

I would love to be able to say Sonja Gorska had grown into a striking woman, but I'd be lying my pants off. The potential for beauty was there. She had strong features, but they were mostly hidden behind that ever-present unibrow. The unstylish glasses didn't help. Neither did that dark hair that was at once mousy and untamed. She wore a long cardigan, at least three sizes too big for her, and a wool skirt despite the balmy spring weather.

"Miss Vanderjadt," she said, cowering as I helped Agatha's walker over the threshold. "Wha-wha-what are you doing here?"

"I *do* live in town," Agatha said. "And these *are* the town archives."

Sonja Gorska clutched a large hardcover volume to her chest. "I know. I'm sorry. I only meant... I heard you didn't get out much, that's all."

"Well, I'm out today."

I tried not to laugh, but I found the unintended double-entendre pretty funny. If Agatha were indeed *out*, the blackmailer's threats would have no impact.

"I'm sorry," Sonja Gorska said. "Thanks for coming. I don't get many visitors on a Sunday."

It would surprise me if she got many visitors at all—apart from schoolchildren dragged to the archives to learn about local history. The space itself was stiflingly small, like a bomb shelter build in the middle ages. It smelled like wet rocks. There were rows of shelving along the walls and another row down the middle. At the back was the archivist's own personal office space.

"Who funds the archives?" I asked, because it seemed like a pretty worthless cause to me.

"Oh," she said. "The town council funds it. They only pay me for three hours a week, but I put in a lot more time than that just because I love it so much. I love the past. I love history. Don't you?"

She'd been a weird girl at school and she'd grown up to be a weird woman.

"How do you pay the bills on three hours' wages?" Agatha asked brusquely.

Pushing her glasses up the bridge of her nose, Sonja said, "Oh, I don't have many expenses. I live with my parents."

Yikes. I knew that was the trend these days, but I didn't understand how any grown person could put up with their parents on a daily basis. Maybe I was just biased by bad experiences.

"You must be saving for something," Agatha pressed. "A house, maybe? Get out of this one-horse town?"

"Oh, no!" Sonja said dreamily. "I would never leave Hillsgrave. I love it here. It's such an interesting place. Do you know how Hillsgrave got its name?"

I felt like I should be able to answer that question. It was the kind of trivia you'd normally find on a diner placemat.

"Miss Vanderjadt?" Sonja asked. "You don't know?"

"I always assumed it was named after a town in England. That's how most places around here got their names."

"Oh, no," Sonja said excitedly. "No, our little town has a much more interesting history. I guess it's my turn to teach you a lesson, Miss. Funny, right? Because you were my teacher and now I'm the one who's..."

When neither I nor Agatha laughed, Sonja Gorska cleared her throat and set the volume she'd been carrying around on a stack of similar books. She led us to the giant map on the wall, but the path was too narrow for Agatha to get her walker through. It got wedged between two solid wooden racks and Agatha wasn't able to retract it on her own.

Sonja Gorska carried on obliviously, giving us a history lesson about the surrounding towns as I led Agatha the other way around the centre rack. When we joined the archivist by the map, she pointed the eraser end of her pencil to a spot down river of Agatha's house.

"In 1881, a businessman from Swiftville decided to expand his enterprise by building a mill."

I watched Agatha's eyes grow wide. I knew exactly what she was thinking when she asked, "A *mill*?"

"That's right," Sonja Gorska said. "Of course, Swiftville is located inland from the river, so we all know the spot he chose for the mill site." To me, she said, "I don't know about you, but when I was a teenager everyone used to party out there in the ruins."

"I'm surprised you got invited to parties," Agatha said to the mousy woman. "You never were much of a looker. Didn't the kids call you Unibrow?"

Sonja's blinked rapidly, and before long her big brown eyes were glistening behind those large glasses. Agatha was very often cruel to me, but I could take it. Someone like Sonja couldn't handle Agatha's brand of malice.

The archivist tittered nervously. Around here, we didn't let our emotions get the best of us.

After grabbing a bottle of water from the low-hanging pocket of her cardigan, Sonja Gorska took a sip, another sip, and then an extended swig. Shame she didn't have a flask in one of those pockets. She could probably use a drink.

Once she'd refreshed her throat, the archivist offered a nervous smile and said, "Sorry about that. It gets so dry in here." She turned back to the map. "As I was saying, Mr. Lawson of Swiftville commissioned the mill to be built on this location. He hired workers—a few men from the area, but mostly men on tramp from the city. The men were paid meagre wages and supplied living quarters and three square meals a day. Back then, that included a staggering amount of beer. Now we drink water, but back then it was beer all the way."

I said, "That's the life," but I don't even drink, so what do I know?

"Well there was a worker of some notoriety who drank more than his fair share," Sonja went on. "He picked fights on the job, passed out drunk, just wasn't what you'd call a reliable worker. When the bosses fired him, unfortunately he had rock pick in hand. He came swinging at his bosses, but another man interceded with a pick of his own and, sadly, the notorious worker perished of his injuries."

"Ouch," I said, because I didn't know how else to react to a story about construction workers from the 1800s slaughtering one of their own.

"The man—a Mr. James Hill—had no family to speak of, and his fellow workers weren't all that fond of him, so they carried his body as far as they could from the mill site. They buried him in loose earth and marked the spot Hill's Grave."

I waited a good ten seconds for the other shoe to drop before realizing it already had. That was the story.

Agatha furrowed her brow. "And that's how our town got its name? After a drunken reprobate who was buried here?"

"Buried approximately where the bank stands today." Sonja pointed out the spot on the map. "I've asked the town council to commission a plaque to commemorate the spot, but they keep telling me it's too expensive."

Letting out an utterly cruel cackle, Agatha said, "Put your head on straight, girl!"

"Agatha," I whispered, hoping she'd soften her tone.

But she didn't. She ignored me and told Sonja Gorska, "Nobody wants to hear a story like that about their town."

Sonja seemed shocked by Agatha's suggestion. "They don't? Why not?"

Before Agatha could insult the archivist with any further flair, I said, "The people of Hillsgrave are proud of their heritage. We get our fair share of tourists through town in the summer months. Who'd want visitors knowing that's how our town got its name? It's gruesome."

Sonja Gorska's expression fell. Tears shone once again in her eyes as she said, "I thought it was a great story. It's got everything: violence, public drunkenness, a mill."

"It's a great story," I assured her. "Just maybe not a great town origin story."

"But I've done so much research to find all this out," she wept. "You have no idea the hours of work..."

Pulling a tissue from her sleeve, she sniffled and croaked and stifled a sob. Agatha looked away, sickened by the show of emotion. I felt bad for Sonja, but I didn't know what to do aside from pat her back and say, "There, there."

That must have worked at least a bit, because a smile flickered across her lips. She bleated, "Thanks."

Agatha glared at me, probably because we'd been here all this time and I hadn't asked about the photographs Max found. It didn't surprise me that Sonja hadn't mentioned them already. But she obviously had her hands full with this drunken mill story. It's possible she hadn't even opened those boxes yet, or put together the AV in the picture with Agatha Vanderjadt, the cranky old schoolteacher.

As Sonja Gorska took another swig from her pocket water bottle, I said, "Actually, Sonja, there's a specific reason we came here today."

"There is?" she asked, sniffling and dabbing at her reddened nose with the tissue.

"There is, yes. We wanted to ask about some pictures and letters you recently received."

She cocked her head and furrowed her brow. "Oh?" she asked, her dry lips forming a perfect O.

I couldn't tell whether she knew what I was talking about, so I said, "They were pictures and letters of an... intimate nature."

"Practically pornographic!" Agatha added.

Sonja Gorska seemed shocked by the suggestion. "Goodness me! No, I certainly haven't seen anything like that!"

"Cut the crap," Agatha growled. "You can play Little Miss Innocent 'til the cows come home, but I'm not buying it. Didn't work in school, and it won't work now."

Sonja's eyes widened until she looked more like a cartoon character than a human person. "I don't know what you mean, Miss Vanderjadt. Please, you mustn't yell at me."

"You call this yelling?!"

I wedged myself between Sonja Gorska and Agatha, half afraid I'd knock the old woman to the ground in the process—and half *hoping* I would. She managed to maintain her footing as I said softly to Sonja, "Maybe there are some boxes that have been donated recently that you haven't fully investigated?"

Sonja Gorska shook her head vigorously. "No, I assure you I look through every donation the archives receives right away. I'm like a kid at Christmas. And anyway, nothing new has come to me in almost a year."

"Ah-ha!" Agatha said. "Caught you in a lie!"

"What lie?" Sonja Gorska asked, seeming utterly confounded.

With a sigh, I said, "Maxine Holdstern told me she brought you some old photographs and letters she found during a renovation project."

Sonja Gorska's face lit up and I thought *all right, back on track!* But instead of mentioning the pictures she asked, "Are you and Max back together? Oh, I'm so happy for you! I always thought you two were a match made in Heaven."

Throwing her arms around me, she gave me an incredibly awkward vice-grip hug. All I could think to say was, "Thanks, Sonja. I didn't realize my relationship with Max was fodder for public inquiry."

"Oh, it isn't," she said as she released me from her grip. "Only, I thought Max was being very closed-minded when she broke up with you just because you decided to live as a man. So what? You were practically a man even when you were a lesbian!"

Part of me wanted to stop her, say *no, it's more complicated than that*, but what I heard myself saying was, "True, I was always pretty butch."

"I'm glad Max finally came to her senses," Sonja went on. "You'll be married within the year. I guarantee it."

"Well, I don't know about that..."

"The pictures!" Agatha growled, obviously losing patience with the discussion of my personal relationship.

"Right," I said. "Sonja, Max told me she brought pictures and letters here to the archives."

"When?" Sonja asked.

"I'm not sure of the date, but fairly recently, I'd say."

Shaking her head in confusion, Sonja said, "I never got any pictures or letters. I'm sorry. I don't know what to tell you."

Max wouldn't have lied about dropping them off here. I mean... why would she lie?

But I'd reached a dead end with Sonja Gorska. All I could think to say was, "Sorry to bother you. Thanks for telling us how Hillsgrave got its name."

"That's it?" Agatha blurted. "You're giving up that easily? What about those pictures? They're here! They've got to be here!"

Pushing past a shocked Sonja Gorska, Agatha entered the woman's private office and began tugging on file cabinet drawers—which wouldn't open.

"Why are these cabinets locked?" Agatha hollered. "What have you got to hide, young lady?"

"They're not locked," Sonja Gorska said in a small and somewhat defeated voice. "You have to push that button on the front while you're pulling. No, push it to the side. No, push the *button* to the side." Shoving her water bottle in her pocket, she closed in on Agatha. "Here, I'll help."

While the mousy archivist convinced Agatha her drawers weren't full of vintage lesbian pornography, I took it upon myself to get the walker unstuck. I didn't drive all the way out to Timbuktu to buy a walker so we could abandon it in the town archives.

Turned out all I had to do was collapse it in on itself and it unstuck immediately.

I waited by the exit door while Agatha sifted through files next to an exasperated archivist. Part of me was obviously curious what had happened to those pictures, but it was hard to cast a net of suspicion over Sonja Gorska. She looked too much like a deer caught in headlights after being struck by lightning. How could she possibly lie to the inimitable Miss Vanderjagt?

If Sonja Gorska said she never received those photos, Sonja Gorksa never received those photos.

But that meant Max must have lied about dropping them off.

And Max would never lie to me.

Would she?

A feeling like heartburn took hold of my chest, and I itched it on the outside, like that was going to do any good. To occupy my mind and get it thinking of anything but blackmail, I read various postings tacked to the bulletin board by the door: ATV for rent or sale (make me an offer), home baking available for home delivery (24 hours' notice please), fashion knits by Nana Vi (specializing in doll clothing, human attire upon request).

Under the bulletin board was a low bookshelf stacked with a variety of flyers. I picked up an order form for the upcoming community theatre season (*No Sex Please, We're British*, followed by *Angels in America, Part One: Millennium Approaches*, and the highlight of every holiday season: *Waiting for Godot~A Christmas Pantomime*). Max would be dying to catch any or all of these productions. They were sure to be stellar.

Another stack of print-outs caught my eye, this time for professional reasons rather than personal ones: *How to Check Your*

Dog for Tics. There had to be a hundred photocopied information sheets.

"Sonja," I called across the narrow archives. "Can I take one of these to post at the kennel?"

She took off her glasses and squinted. "The tics thing? Take a whole stack. You've got a more captive audience of dog owners there than I have here."

Agatha had managed to make a disaster zone of Sonja Gorska's office with nothing to show for it. Grumbling, she said, "You've won this round, Little Miss Innocent, but I know you've got a trick or two up that sleeve."

From what I'd observed, Sonja Gorska's sleeves were stuffed with tissues. Not really sure how she'd manage to shove any tricks up there.

Agatha made her way down the narrow row by balancing herself between sturdy racks of archival materials. Sonja Gorska held the door for her while I helped her manoeuvre the walker outside. She first thanked the archivist for the assistance and then gruffly added, "You haven't seen the last of us."

Puzzled, Sonja Gorska said, "My pleasure. Come back any time—except Mondays and Tuesdays. We're closed Mondays and Tuesdays."

I tossed the tics printouts and the community theatre order form between the two front seats, and then helped Agatha into the van—which she complained was far too high off the ground for any sensible person to get into. Then I folded up her walker and parked it in the back.

She was complaining about the dog smell when I got into the driver's seat, and without thinking I snapped, "Do you really have to behave this way?"

Her lips glued shut momentarily, but she quickly responded with: "What way?"

"The way you treat people." I didn't want to be saying any of this, but I couldn't hold back. "You treat me like a servant, take everything I do for granted, you bark at Sonja Gorska when we're trying to get information out of her..."

"Well, the girl was obviously lying."

"How do you figure?"

"She had to be lying!"

"I really don't think she was, Agatha, and even if you're right haven't you ever heard you catch more flies with honey?"

Ignoring that particular comment, Agatha said, "If Little Miss Innocent is telling the truth, that means your lady-friend is lying. How do you like them apples?"

That heartburn feeling filled my chest again, and I scratched but it didn't go away. "Max wouldn't lie to me."

"She broke up with you for living as a man, but nooo she'd never lie."

"Exactly," I said calmly even though the memory made me want to put my fist through the windshield. "Max never lied to me, even when the going got tough. She confronts things head-on. That's my Max."

"That's not what I heard," Agatha mumbled.

I knew exactly what she'd said, but I played dumb—literally—and asked, "What'd you just say?"

Agatha shrugged. "Oh nothing."

"Don't you *oh nothing* me. Tell me what you heard."

With a holier-than-thou expression painted across her wrinkled old face, Agatha told me, "Scuttlebutt had it Maxine was going around with someone else even while you two were still together."

I gripped the wheel until my knuckles turned white. Good thing I hadn't turned the key in the ignition yet, or I'd have probably run my van through the archives building.

Agatha added, "I hate to be the bearer of bad news."

"You love to be the bearer of bad news," I barked like a riled-up Doberman. "But guess what? I already knew Max cheated on me. She told me herself and we worked through it like the sensible adults we are, so in your face, old lady. You lose this round of *let's hurt people's feelings for no good reason*."

"Still doesn't make up for ending the relationship because of your transition."

My jaw locked. I could barely open it to say, "She apologized for that—apologized profusely."

"It's your life," Agatha replied. "Only you can choose which trespasses to forgive."

"You just want everyone to die alone, as miserable as you are!"

That might have been a step too far, because Agatha made no reply.

I couldn't read the expression on her face, because I couldn't bring myself to look at her.

Starting up the car, I drove as fast as my jittery feet would take me. I didn't say a word the whole way back to the house. When we got there, I parked at top speed, ripped her walker out of the back, got her out of the van, and guided her around back and in through the kitchen.

I walked through her house without taking off my boots. When I got to the front door, I said, "Time's running out, old lady.

Your blackmailer wants that money tomorrow, if I'm not mistaken. Better get to the bank early. It's quite a bus trip out to the mill."

"Bus trip?" Agatha asked, seeming mortified by the idea of public transportation.

"Yup," I said, looking up at her from the base of the stairs. "The intertown bus stops outside the bank around noon. It's only one stop to the old mill site. But make sure to get back to the bus stop by four or you'll be stuck out there overnight."

I waited for her to say she expected me to take the day off work to chauffeur her out there, but instead she said, "You're the one who old me not to pay. You said we'd find the blackmailer."

"Yeah, but we didn't," I spat. "Instead you decided to take me down a notch with that comment about Max. We just got back together and already you're trying to break us up. Why? So you can have me all to yourself? You think if I'm in a relationship I won't have any time for you? Well, maybe you're right, Agatha. Maybe I've done all I can do here. Maybe you're beyond helping."

As I slammed the door behind me, I heard her call out, "Wait!"

And I did, just for a second. I clung to that door handle thinking I really ought to go back in and fix her something for supper.

But instead, I let go. I left her alone. Maybe forever.

Chapter Eight

I didn't think Max would be working on a Sunday, but when I got to her house no one was home. That made me nervous and I don't know why. A bunch of thoughts kept racing through my mind: questioning Sonja Gorska, questioning Max, even questioning Agatha.

Sure Sonja Gorska played the innocent, but according to Agatha it was an act she didn't buy—just like the town council wouldn't buy that plaque Sonja wanted for the drunken mill worker's gravesite. Maybe those pictures of a young Agatha Vanderjadt frolicking with her lesbian lover set off a lightbulb in Sonja Gorska's mind: she could fund the plaque herself by blackmailing the two women. Except one of them was dead. Only Agatha remained.

On the other hand, it was entirely possible Agatha had invented this whole blackmail situation. I know that seems unlikely, but just look at how much time I'd devoted to her this weekend: pretty much my every waking hour.

Well, except Saturday night, which I spent with Max.

And Sunday afternoon, which I spent waiting for Max.

It was nearly four when her truck rounded the bend. She slowed when she spotted my van, then parked quickly on the street since I was already in her driveway.

"Oh my God, Chris! What are you doing here?" In the time it took me to hop down from the driver's seat, she'd raced up the driveway and wrapped her arms around my waist. "I'm so happy to see you! Sorry, I smell."

"No," I told her. "That's the van. Smells like dogs."

"No, it's me." She sniffed her pits. "I forgot to put on deodorant this morning. That's your fault. You make me loopy!"

She smacked my chest playfully. I don't know if I'm hypersensitive or she's super-strong, but it actually kind of hurt.

"Those picture of Agatha—you said you donated them to the archives."

Max's expression fell, probably because she was being so playful and there I was in serious mode.

"Yeah," she said. "I did. What's this about?"

"I talked to Sonja Gorska. She said she never got any photos or letters. She said she hasn't received any sort of donations in almost a year."

Max scrunched up her face, crossed her arms in front of her chest. "Are you calling me a liar?"

"I don't know. Are you lying?"

"No, I'm not lying. Why would I lie?"

"I don't know, Max. But someone's blackmailing the woman in those photos, and you're the only one I've come across who's been willing to admit you've even seen them. What am I supposed to think?"

"You're supposed to think I'm telling the truth, because I *am* telling the truth!"

You'd think Max would be concerned about the neighbours overhearing all this, but apparently not. A pink glow moved up her neck and into her cheeks as she shouted her head off, asking, "What do you want, a signed affidavit? Want me to write it in blood? What?"

I grabbed her arms and pulled her close and kissed her. Don't ask me why. Or do ask, and I'll tell you it's because Max is gorgeous when she's angry. But I wouldn't tell her that. It would only make her angrier. A vicious circle of beauty and rage.

At first she started to pull away, but I didn't let go and she soon melted into me, wrapping her angry arms around me and clutching my back—not that I could feel much through my binder. Damn thing really gets tight when my breathing gets rapid.

She backed off and said, "Sorry."

"For what?"

"For shouting at you. For saying what I said."

"Remind me... what'd you say?"

Max rolled her eyes and smiled. "You really are a guy."

Even if she intended that as a mild criticism, I took it as the highest compliment.

"You asked if I really donated all those pictures of Agatha and Martha to the archives, and I said I did. Ringing any bells?"

"Oh yeah." *That's why I came here in the first place. Right.* "Sorry, I just got distracted by your... by... you know, you look incredibly hot with your cheeks all flaming red like that."

Max covered her cheeks with both hands. "Pay attention, Chris. You called me a liar and I can't say I'm pleased about it. But we'll talk this through like adults. What makes you think I would lie to you?"

My mind reeled. All I could think about was stripping off her smelly T-shirt and throwing her in the shower. Or maybe just stripping off the cargo pants and hosing her down. If she left the T-shirt on, it would get all wet and stick to her skin and...

"Chris, are you even listening?"

"Huh?"

"Would you please stop staring at my boobs?"

"What? I wasn't."

A loving smirk spread across Max's lips as she shook her head gently. "You said you talked to Sonja Gorska at the archives and she never got the pictures."

"Oh. That's right."

"Or the letters?"

"No pictures, no letters. But if you say you gave them to her of course I believe you, Max. She could be lying for any number of reasons."

"Or not," Max suggested.

"Well someone's gotta be lying."

"Not necessarily, Chris."

Either I missed something or I was even more distracted by mental images of Max in a wet T-shirt. "I don't get it. Either you gave her the stuff and she's saying you didn't—in which case she's lying—or you never gave her the stuff, in which case..."

"I never gave it to her," Max said.

"But I thought..."

"I took the boxes of pictures and the shoebox of letters to the archives, but it's not like I put them directly in her hands. It was afterhours by the time I got there, so I left everything outside the door. I figured who's gonna steal a couple boxes? But you never know. Maybe someone did."

I could feel my whole body slumping. If some random passerby picked up those photos of Agatha and Martha, then every resident of Hillsgrave was now a suspect.

Back to the drawing board.

"When you said you donated them to the archives, I just assumed you put them in the archivist's hands."

With a shrug, Max said, "You know what they say about assumptions."

I gave her a playful shove and she shoved me back and I leaned in to kiss her but at the same time she reached into my van. "Hey, I want to see this!"

She yanked the community theatre flyer from between the seats.

"Oh, yeah, I figured you would. That's why I picked up the order form. I thought we could pick some dates, go together."

Max seemed incredibly impressed. "Suddenly you're willing to see community theatre productions?"

"Well, you know what they say. Relationships are all about sacrifice. I'm not sure how they plan to do *Waiting for Godot* as a pantomime, but I'm willing to find out."

"Awww, my hero!" Leaning close, she kissed me sweetly on the cheek. Then she dove back into the van, pulling out the stack of tic print-outs. "What other goodies have you got for me?"

"Oh, I grabbed those to hand out at the kennel."

"Boring," she said, and tossed them on the driver's seat. But as she did, a piece of paper folded into thirds fluttered to her feet. "What's this?"

"You tell me."

When she unfolded it and I realized what she had in hand, I was overcome by a strange sort of embarrassment. It was Agatha's blackmail letter. God only knows how it ended up in my van. Agatha must have brought it along when we visited the archives. I guess it fell out of her purse and she didn't notice.

Anyway, the idea of Max reading those words made me weirdly uncomfortable. I felt like I was betraying Agatha by allowing Max to read it. But it's not like I could grab the thing out of her hands. Anyway, I'd already told Max all about the situation at dinner last night.

"Poor Miss Vanderjadt! Where will she get this amount of money in one day? Does she have it?"

"In the bank, I think."

"Are you driving her out to the old mill to make the drop?"

Averting Max's gaze, I said, "I've got a shift at the kennel."

"So? Take the day off. Take an hour off. She obviously relies on you."

"Yeah, I know she does. Too much, maybe."

"Chris, she's just an old lady. You're the one who's always complaining how the younger generations abandon our elders. And queer elders, even more so!"

"Yeah, okay, I get it."

"If you really can't take her, I can slip away from the jobsite for an hour or two."

"No," I said. "It's fine. I'll do it. She trusts me."

Max seemed oblivious to how irritated I was.

One of the tic print-outs slipped off the seat and Max managed to grab it before it even hit the driveway. I closed the door so no more papers could fly out. When Max went back to reading the blackmail letter, she laughed out loud.

"What's so funny?"

"Oh, I'm looking at the wrong sheet. *Removing a tick is easy as Parcheesi.* My mind's going, like, why's a blackmail letter suddenly talking about tics?" As Max looked from the letter to the print-out, her brow furrowed. "Chris, did you notice this?"

She held the sheets side by side like my van was a giant refrigerator and her hands were a pair of magnets.

As soon as she asked the question I knew what she was talking about, but no, I hadn't noticed it before that moment.

"I gotta go," I said, swiping the blackmail letter from her hand and opening the driver's side door.

"Go where?" she asked, backing away from the van. "Want me to come?"

I should have answered, but I was too focused on what I had to do. I tossed the stack of printouts between the seats, hopped in, and started the engine.

"Chris!" she called as I closed the door. "Don't do anything stupid. Promise me!"

"I won't," I assured her as I backed out of the driveway. But even I didn't believe that.

Chapter Nine

Sonja Gorska was closing up shop as I pulled in outside the archives. When I swung open the van door, she jumped, throwing both arms in the air the way robbers do in old-time movies.

"Oh," she said, pressing one hand to her heart. "It's just you. That van, you know, it *is* rather imposing."

"Don't play innocent with me," I shot back. "I know you're behind all this."

"Behind all what?" she asked, picking up the keys she'd dropped.

"All *this*," I said, shoving the blackmail letter in her face.

Sonja Gorska squinted at the paper. Unravelling a pair of glasses stuck in her hair, she set them squarely on her nose. She grabbed the letter out of my hand and startled noticeably as she read it. "This is why you came by with Miss Vanderjadt earlier today? Goodness, who would do such a thing? Blackmailing the elderly! How very ungenerous."

"I think we both know who sent this letter."

She looked up at me like an owl, asking, "Who?"

"Who? You!"

Her owl eyes widened as she bobbed her head back. "Me? I would never do a thing like this."

Grabbing one of the tic printouts, I said, "If you didn't send that blackmail letter, why does it have the exact same smudge in the exact same spot as these printouts I took from your archives? Obviously your printer's got a spot on the glass. It showed up when you printed these tic leaflets, just like it showed up when you printed that blackmail letter."

"But I didn't print those leaflets, just like I didn't print this blackmail demand. Miss Vanderjadt was horrid to me, but I've come to realize people are only horrid when they're unhappy. If anything, I feel sorry for the woman."

"Wait, wait, wait—back up. You didn't print these leaflets?"

She blinked her owl eyes and said, "No."

"But they were in your archives."

"That's right. Someone brought them 'round."

"Someone?" I asked. "What someone? Who?"

"Oh, he was... what was his name?"

"You tell me!"

"It's on the tip of my tongue. He came in and asked if he could leave the stack of... well, isn't there any contact information on it?"

"No," I said, scanning it again even though I already knew the answer. "It's just information about spotting and removing tics."

"Yes, we talked about that. He went on and on about his dogs. He had... oh, what are they called? I'm more of a cat person."

"I don't know! I don't know! Golden retrievers?"

"No..."

"Labradors—labs—black labs, golden labs."

"No, it wasn't Labradors."

"Poodles? Doberman? Terriers? Corgis?"

"Yes!"

"Corgis?"

"No, terriers—I remember him telling me they were originally bred to kill rats in factories and I thought well I must have the wrong breed in mind because terriers look so tiny and sweet."

"Terriers?" I asked, searching my mental catalogue of terrier owners in town. "Was it Mike Johansen? He's got a Jack Russell."

"I don't think so, no. This man was here on business. I believe that's what he said."

"Business? Who comes to Hillsgrave on business?"

Sonja Gorska's eyes widened as she extended the blackmail letter in my direction. "Unless he meant... you don't think *blackmail* was his business?"

"I don't know! Who is this guy? Think, Sonja: what did he look like?"

"Bald," she said. "The kind of man who gives you a bit of a shiver. I remember thinking he had the same name as a dragon."

"A dragon? Oh, that helps!"

"No, I mean—" An expression of glee overtook the mousy archivist, and she threw her finger in the air, a Eureka moment. "O'Leary! Damian O'Leary."

"Damon O'Leary? The real estate agent?"

Sonja Gorska's brow furrowed slightly. "He might have mentioned real estate. I don't really remember. He only talked about his dogs and about tics."

"He grew up here in town. He went to our school. He was older."

She shrugged. "If you say so."

"And he's the one who brought you this whole stack of print-outs?"

"Yes, that's what I've been telling you!"

I fished through the gap between the two front seats until I found what I was looking for: the print-out that slick shyster Damon O'Leary had handed me at the open house.

"What's that?" the archivist asked.

"Damon O'Leary is selling his parents' house here in Hillsgrave. This is the spec sheet he gave me when I checked it out with Agatha."

Sonja Gorska pointed to the smudge on the open house sheet. It matched the smudge on the blackmail letter and the one on the tic printout. "Look! It's got the same mark. I think you've figured out who your blackmailer is."

Snatching the blackmail letter a little too roughly from the archivist's grasp, I said, "I need to tell Agatha."

The mousy woman smiled understandingly, and for a second I thought I should probably apologize for accusing her of blackmail. But apologies were never my strong suit, so I hopped in the van, waved goodbye, and put the pedal to the metal.

I kept thinking how relieved Agatha would be that I'd figured out who her blackmailer was, but halfway to her house I realized solving the mystery didn't resolve the problem. So I knew it was Damon O'Leary who was extorting her. So what? He still had in his possession pictures and information, and likely letters too, that Agatha didn't want falling into the wrong hands.

He could just as easily blackmail her face to face as he could in secret.

Afternoon gave way to evening as I approached Agatha's house. I was just slowing down to turn into her driveway when I realized... *hey wait... there's another car already parked there*. A black luxury vehicle—the sort of thing you didn't often see in Hillsgrave.

Spotting that car outside Agatha's house turned my intestines to ice. I overshot her driveway, continuing on down her street and finally parking at the side of the road.

Someone was in there with Agatha, and I knew in my gut she wasn't safe.

Chapter Ten

My legs turned into a pair of gummy worms as I backtracked along Agatha's street. Her living room was dark, which wasn't the norm at this time of day. Usually she'd be visible from the sidewalk, sitting in her recliner with her eyes glued to the TV.

The luxury vehicle must belong to Damon O'Leary. Who else but a slimy real estate agent would drive around Hillsgrave in a car like that? When I glanced in the dark windows, I could just make out spec sheets for his parents' house on the passenger seat. He must have come to Agatha's after Sunday's open house.

I guess he just couldn't wait for that money.

As I approached the house quiet as a mouse, the only light I could see came from somewhere toward the back. If I entered through the front door, I'd give Damon O'Leary a heads-up that someone was around. He'd have an opportunity to flee. Or worse.

So instead of going in the front door, I quietly unlatched the gate and slipped around back.

When I got to the patio area, where only yesterday I'd brought Agatha her battery-powered radio and the photocopies that had arrived in the mail, I stayed behind the lattice wall where morning glories would grow in a few months' time. Through the lattice, I could see directly into the illuminated kitchen. The door was open, and through the screen door I spotted Damon O'Leary pacing the floor, knife in hand.

Oh God, where was Agatha? What had he done to her?

But the knife wasn't bloody. It was one from Agatha's set, perfectly clean and shiny, just the way I'd left it after washing her dishes.

My arms were dead weight, but my hands wouldn't stop trembling. I knew I had to act. My body wouldn't listen. Every muscle locked as I stared through the lattice. My hearing became so focused I'm sure I could hear a pin drop five houses over.

A wave of relief washed over me when I heard Agatha saying, "Let me get this straight: you and that woman contractor who renovated your parents' house—you were in it together?"

My chest seized before Damon O'Leary let out a callous burst of laughter. "Me? Team up with that dumb dyke? No way! Maxine's too soft-hearted to pull off a caper like this."

I was relieved to hear him say Max wasn't involved, but when some shifty townie calls your girl a dumb dyke, let me tell you, it really gets your blood boiling.

"Then how did you get your dirty paws on my pictures?" Agatha asked. "She must have brought them to you."

"Only because I was her client and the house belonged to my folks. She told me all about these letters and photographs, said she found your love story fascinating. I thought the whole thing was revolting—revolting, and titillating in its way—but I played along. I convinced the lass your photos and words were historically valuable, advised her to donate the lot to the town archives."

"You had no right," Agatha spat as I made my way nervously around the lattice. "No right whatsoever to give away what was rightfully mine!"

"Oh, it was all a set-up anyway. Haven't you figured that out yet? I'd been to the archives to drop off flyers. I knew they were closed on Mondays and Tuesdays. And then the dumb dyke didn't deliver those boxes until after dark anyway! I tell you, she might as well have been in on the plot. She made it that easy for me. All I had to do was wait nearby. As soon as she'd dumped the boxes, I picked them up. Easy as Parcheesi!"

My heart hammered so loudly I almost couldn't make out all the insults Agatha hurled at Damon O'Leary. And I was nervous for good reason: all the real estate agent had to do was glance out the screen door and he'd see me standing there, watching him. He wielded that knife like he had no trepidations about driving it through an elderly woman's heart.

I could only hope that, because all the windows on the screen door were currently in the closed position, if he glanced outside he would only see the kitchen reflected in glass. It was dark outside, and the kitchen was brightly lit. Fingers crossed he wouldn't know I was there.

When I snuck even closer to the kitchen door, Agatha was saying, "Tell the world for all I care! I will not be bullied by the likes of you!"

"The Great and Powerful *Demon* O'Leary doesn't frighten you?" he asked. "That's what you used to call me in school, remember? *Demon O'Leary?*"

"Oh, I remember," Agatha said. "I remember very well."

When I peeked in the screen door, I could just make out Damon O'Leary's back: same fancy suit he'd worn the previous day, shining ever so slightly under Agatha's kitchen light.

I couldn't see Agatha herself. She must have been seated in one of the kitchen chairs. But I could certainly hear her as she added, "*Demon* is only the name *I* called you. I also remember how the other children addressed you on the playground."

"Shut up!" the real estate agent cried, practically screeching the words as he waved the kitchen knife side to side. "Don't say it, old lady. I'll cut you! I will!"

Clearly, he underestimated Agatha's fearlessness. Without pause, she said, "*Diaper* O'Leary. That's what they called you after you peed in your pants. From that day forward, it was always Diaper O'Leary in the schoolyard."

Her words must have struck him like a punch, because he stumbled back far enough to give me a clear view of Agatha. She wasn't merely sitting in one of her kitchen chairs—she was strapped to it! A roll of duct tape sat on the kitchen table, used up nearly down to the cardboard centre. Damon O'Leary had wrapped almost the entire roll around Agatha's torso, securing her to the seat.

When I saw what that man had done, it made me the worst combination of angry and sick. Part of me wanted to throw up, but another part prepared to spring into action.

"You'll always be a little demon to me," Agatha sneered. "But to the rest of this town, you're Diaper O'Leary. That's why you left, isn't it?"

"Shut your wicked mouth!" Damon O'Leary shouted. The big knife shook in his hand as he pointed it from across the room. He looked like he was gearing up to take a run at the old woman. "I'm a huge success. That's why I went to the city: to build an umpire!"

"If you're such a success, why are you blackmailing old ladies? Perhaps your *umpire* isn't as profitable as you'd like us to believe."

"The city's not cheap," he stammered self-righteously. "You try paying the rent on a real estate office in the right part of town, all while wearing the right suit, the perfect shoes, wining and dining potential clients. It costs an arm and a half!"

"So your great success is all an act," Agatha replied with a callous chuckle. "You're still Diaper O'Leary and you always will be."

I'd pretty much convinced myself Damon O'Leary was all talk and no action. He wouldn't hurt Agatha. But that last bit really set him off. Anger flashed across his face, and he suddenly looked possessed—truly demonic!

Aiming the knife at Agatha, he set off like an enraged bull set on sticking his horns straight through the old lady's chest.

I flew at the screen door, hoping to God neither Agatha nor Damon had flipped the lock. Maybe it was the lucky four-leafed clover in my wallet, I don't know, but the door flew open with my weight firmly behind it. Damon O'Leary crashed into the glass, knife and all.

With the speed at which he was running, you'd think that glass would shatter all over the floor... but it didn't. His head bashed the pane with an unsettlingly hollow smack. Down he went, knife in hand.

"You sure took your time," Agatha grumbled.

I didn't get a chance to return the volley. Damon O'Leary was flat on his back on the kitchen floor, mumbling incomprehensibly. I could practically hear the little tweety birds circling his head. He was down, but not out. As long as that knife was in his hand, he was a threat.

Just as his grip tightened around the handle, I stomped over and smashed the heel of my boot on his wrist. He cried out in pain, but released his hold on the knife handle.

"Finally those darn boots come in handy," Agatha groaned.

I thought I was in the clear, but as I reached down to pick up the knife, Damon O'Leary's other hand came flying at my leg. He grabbed me hard, right around the pocket of my cargo pants. Agatha jumped when a crunching noise rang through the kitchen.

"Let Chris go!" Agatha cried. "Don't hurt him, you wretch!"

At the same time, Damon said, "Are your pants full of cereal?"

"Doggie treats."

"In your pants?" Agatha asked.

"Just the pockets."

Damon grabbed my leg again, just below the pocket. It scared the bejesus out of me, but I played it cool and said, "I think you're forgetting who's holding the knife."

He started to raise his head off the floor, then winced. "I'm not forgetting anything," he said, in this heavy, threatening tone that spoke to my deepest fears. "I remember more than I let on."

I knew what he was getting at. At least, I think I did.

But so what? So what if he knew me when I was a kid? He could think, say, feel whatever he wanted about me. Didn't change who I was. Not one bit.

"You're lucky I'm a gentleman," he said in that slimy tone of voice men use exclusively to threaten women.

Without really thinking, I kicked him in the chin. I wasn't exactly trying to break his jaw, but I wasn't exactly trying not to.

It hadn't occurred to me that, when I lifted one boot off the floor, I'd be setting all my weight on the other—which was conveniently located on Damon O'Leary's wrist. So it's possible I broke that too. Again, not what I was going for, but considering he'd duct taped Agatha to a chair and was about to run a knife through her heart, this was probably a suitable punishment.

I'd almost forgotten about that roll of duct tape on the table. There was still some silvery tape left, so I set the knife down and grabbed the roll instead. There was something very gratifying about that zippery sound when you tear at tape and it unsticks from itself.

Damon O'Leary must have thought so too, because he heaved up from the floor like a zombie rising from the grave, one hand waving limply as he reached for me. Only made it easier to wrap duct tape around both his arms.

He screamed—in pain, I thought, until he cried out, "You've ruined the nap! This jacket is lamb's wool, you cretin!"

"Sorry about that." I wrapped yet more duct tape around his hands.

There wasn't enough left on the roll for me to tape his ankles together, but with his arms secured in front of him and one wrist more than likely broken, I was pretty sure he wouldn't be able to get up off the floor.

"Don't mind me," Agatha grumbled. "I'm only tied to a chair."

"Oh, quit your complaining. I saved your life, didn't I?"

Without meeting my gaze, she said, "I guess..."

Just for that, I picked up the phone instead of freeing her first. Anyway, peeling all the duct tape from her wrinkly skin was going to be a delicate procedure.

It was Damon O'Leary who said, "What's the phone for?"

"For calling the police. What do you think?"

"Ahh, but if you call the police you'll have to tell them why I was here. They'll find out all about those racy photographs and your sordid affair. It was my impression you didn't want a living soul to know about your youthful indiscretions, Miss Vanderjagt."

When I looked to Agatha, her expression read as solemn and resigned. Still without looking me in the eye, she said, "Make the call."

Chapter Eleven

"How's that stair lift coming along?" Agatha asked as I opened Max's laptop at her kitchen table.

"You heard what Max said: she'll let you know when it's ready for a test run."

Agatha didn't seem to notice what was on the computer right in front of her. In fact, she peeked over the screen, casting her gaze toward the front stairs where Max drilled a track into the wall.

In a ridiculous stage-whisper, Agatha said, "That girlfriend of yours sure is taking her time."

"Taking her time? She's been at it ten minutes!"

From across the house, Max met my gaze with a sympathetic smirk. She showed Agatha more patience than I ever could.

Pulling up a chair next to the old lady, I tried again to draw her attention to the laptop. "Look at this, Agatha. It's the website we talked about. Max did an amazing job putting it together. See? The homepage is the introduction you wrote, along with an adult content warning. People can click here to see the pictures of you and Martha, and they can click here to read the letters. Max scanned it all and uploaded it for you. Didn't she do a great job?"

I expected Agatha to make some crabby comment about the site, but she didn't say anything at all. In fact, when I started scrolling through her love letters to Martha, she stopped me. I watched her eyes darting across the screen. As she read them over, a faint smile drew across her lips. Her expression seemed distant, like she was seeing the life she'd once lived.

The sound of Max's drill shook her back into the present.

"Well?" I asked eagerly. "What do you think?"

"The font's a little. And this heading should be bigger." She clicked the link that led to the photo section, and sighed as she scrolled through the images. "Hard to believe I was ever that young."

"I think you made the right choice," I told her. "Nobody can hold your past against you if you don't hold it against yourself."

Agatha nodded slowly. "This way, the younger queers will see documented proof that lesbians existed long before they were born. And if some people don't like it?" Agatha waved a hand dismissively. "If they don't like it, they don't have to look."

What an incredible change in attitude. The day Agatha received Damon O'Leary's blackmail letter, she was shaking in her boots, not wanting a soul to find out Martha had been the love of her life. Just look at her now, sharing her words, sharing her image with the world!

"It's a good thing Damon O'Leary didn't destroy the photos and letters," I said.

"Why would he?" Agatha asked. "Then he'd have nothing to hold against me."

"True."

Max swore at the wall as she worked at putting up the stair lift.

"Do you need a hand over there?" I asked.

"No, I'm fine," she said before going back to drilling.

"There's one thing I've been wondering about," I said to Agatha.

"What?" she shouted over the racket. "I can't hear a word you're saying."

Max stopped drilling long enough for me to say, "I kept meaning to ask you why Damon O'Leary came to your house in the first place. The drop date hadn't passed yet. You were supposed to bring the money to the mill the following day. So why did he tie you up and threaten you?"

"I thought I told you all this," Agatha replied grumpily. "Maybe I'm thinking of the police. Anyway, the little demon thought we were on to him. When we showed up at the open house, that put him on edge. Figured I knew he was the one blackmailing me."

"Which you didn't—not at that point."

"Nope, but it was enough that he started following us around—us together and you on your own."

The thought of Damon O'Leary watching my every move made me shudder. "He was following me? I didn't notice. That's kind of freaky."

"Yeah, he saw you meet up with his contractor and thought she must have told you it was his idea to donate my photos and letters to the archives. In his mind, our visit to the archives confirmed his suspicions."

"So he showed up at your house with all the blackmail fodder and demanded money on the spot?"

"He figured I already knew it was him, thought I'd go to the police if I had a chance to sleep on it."

"But you didn't know he was the blackmailer—you didn't know until he told you."

"And I laughed in his face! That's what really set him off. Damon O'Leary doesn't like being laughed at, never did, not even as a child. That man's got a chip on his shoulder the size of Mount Kilimanjaro."

"So maybe laughing at him wasn't the best choice."

Agatha didn't seem too concerned. "I wasn't giving Diaper O'Leary one red cent! Bad enough he'd seen those photos of me in the altogether."

I couldn't help shaking my head. Agatha Vanderjadt was one stubborn broad. She had a mouth on her that nearly got her stabbed to death, and she didn't seem concerned in the least. Gave her no reason to change her attitude.

Although, she'd obviously changed in one regard: she didn't mind seeing nude pictures of herself posted on the internet. Not just that, but it was her idea! I kept asking her, "Do you realize the entire world will be able to see this site?" She nodded resolutely and told me the shame of it had held her back her whole life. She realized now she was too darn old not to be proud of who she was.

A piece of news popped into my head and I said, "Hey, you know what Max told me?"

"Hay is for horses," Agatha grumbled. "What did Max tell you?"

"You know that house we looked at—the one where Martha and Joseph lived?"

"The two of you are buying it and moving in together?" Agatha eagerly replied. "Better yet, getting married!"

I glanced quickly in Max's direction to make sure she hadn't heard. "Sheesh, we only just started dating again! No, it turns out Damon O'Leary's parents never wanted to sell. He strong-armed them into moving into an old folks' home. They really wanted to stay in their own house, and now they get to do just that—live in a beautifully renovated version of home. Max says they're over the moon. We're gonna help them move their stuff back in."

Agatha didn't seem to care much about the good news of relative strangers, and I'm not sure why I expected her to be. She hadn't changed *that* much.

"Okay!" Max called from the front steps. "I think we're good to go. Miss Vanderjadt, are you ready to take your inaugural ride?"

I don't know how Max had managed to put up the tracks and assemble the lift so fast, but Max never ceased to amaze me. We'd been through a lot in our time, and it felt great to finally be back together. When we weren't a couple, I always felt like a part of me was missing.

"We'll have to get you a second walker," I told Agatha. "You can keep one on the landing down there and use it when you leave the house."

"I've got another model in mind," she replied as she wheeled out of the kitchen. "The flyer's on the fridge, there. You can pick it up any day this week."

Rolling my eyes, I said, "Your wish is my command."

As I watched Max instruct the always-impatient Agatha how to use her new chair lift, I couldn't stop thinking how lucky I was. I had a girlfriend to love, a fun job playing with dogs, and an old lady to drive me crazy. That's right: I had it all.

The End

The Turkey Wore Satin

A Thanksgiving Tale of Murder, Mystery, and Men in Women's Clothing!

Chapter One

The first year Marty joined Kristin's family for Thanksgiving dinner, he thought they were all a bunch of lunatics.

Not much had changed since that day four years ago, except that Marty was no longer Kristin's puppy-love boyfriend. After a big summer wedding, he was now officially her faithful husband. And, as an official member of the Mayfair family, this year Marty would take part in one of the illustrious family's long-standing traditions: The Amazing Annual Mayfair Family Drag Show.

Kristin's elegantly coifed grandmother Iris, who had buried no fewer than four husbands, explained the family drag show with great fanfare the first time Marty dined at her impressive mansion. It started in the 1940s, not long before Iris's brothers were killed storming the beaches of Normandy.

One Thanksgiving, after a lean wartime dinner, young Iris played her favourite song for the family: *Don't Sit Under the Apple Tree*. The boys were not great fans of the Andrews Sisters—not that they would admit, at any rate—but in lieu of their normal teases, Iris's brothers put on a show. They all got up and sang along, and Mayfair Family History was made.

The impromptu lip-synch marked the beginning of an annual tradition to honour three fallen soldiers. Iris could imagine no better way to show gratitude for their sacrifice than to insist all men in the Mayfair family get gussied up in women's clothing every year on Thanksgiving Day. Her late brothers had a fine sense of humour, she told Marty. They'd have loved it every bit as much as she did.

From humble beginnings, the tradition grew year by year. Nowadays, every man chose a female celebrity to impersonate. It cost a pretty penny, too. In the weeks leading up to the great event, every man went out to buy flash and glam costumes, wigs, and the glitziest makeup on the shelf.

Kristin wore makeup, sure, but barely more than a touch of rosy lipstick and a subdued shade of eye shadow. No use raiding her makeup cache. Tyrone was kind enough to take Marty under his wing, since this was his first performance. They went out together, to a theatrical supplies store, to pick up golden eye shadow and fake lashes with sparkles built right in! The price of it all blew Marty away—not that anyone in the Mayfair family seemed concerned about money.

In fact, even when Grandma Iris had told him the story of the first wartime drag show, he couldn't help wondering if the austerity measures she spoke of amounted to little more than enjoying five courses instead of seven. Maybe only three kinds of pie instead of eight.

"Are you ready for this?" Tyrone asked as he strapped Marty into a vintage Madonna cone bra. "Competition can get pretty intense. The Mayfair men are cut throat when it comes to winning Best in Show."

Tyrone was another Mayfair in-law, married to Grandma Iris's son Jonnie. Every year, he performed as Tina Turner. He had the perfect complexion for it, not to mention the perfect legs. Marty didn't usually notice other men's legs, but by the time Tyrone suited up in a shimmering magenta dress, tossed on a wig, and perfected his make-up, you'd have thought he was Tina herself. Rumour had it he'd performed professionally in his younger days, which he absolutely denied, since it would have barred him from the family competition.

And Marty was getting a real sense of how fierce this competition could be!

As far as Marty was concerned, Tyrone could be called the best of the bunch. At first, he'd attributed the guy's killer performance to the whole being gay thing. But if that were the case, Jonnie would have been a shoe-in for drag, too—and it turned out Jonnie was the biggest flop of them all. Anyway, according to Kristin, Tyrone had never won Best in Show. Imagine that! He was obviously cream of the crop.

Maybe the game was fixed?

Nah, couldn't be. First off, who would go to all the trouble of rigging a family drag competition? And, secondly, it was the Mayfair women who voted on the best performance. They always picked the most bumbling, fumbling, silly performer: Uncle George, a Mayfair by marriage who always snagged the role of Bette Midler. They probably just picked him so he wouldn't feel too humiliated.

Marty wasn't exactly in it to win it, but surely he could count on one woman's vote.

"My wife will definitely pick me," Marty said as Tyrone helped him with his headpiece: a platinum blonde wig he and Kristen had braided and then wrapped around a Styrofoam cone. "That still sounds weird, to me: my wife. *My wife* is going to vote for me in the Amazing Annual Mayfair Family Drag Show."

Tyrone chuckled, but he was swiftly interrupted by gravelly laughter from Marty's father-in-law.

"Don't count on it," said Jack, who'd already slipped into on a slinky black dress. "Kristin always votes for her good old dad. Just because she's got herself a *first* husband doesn't mean she's going to change her loyalties."

"Uhhh okay," Marty replied, trying desperately not to stare at the man's shiny bald head, not to mention the bulge down south. "I only figured, you know, since we just got married a couple months ago, Kristin might vote for me this year."

Jack laughed crassly. "Wait and see, buddy-boy."

"Leave the kid alone," said Uncle George, who looked more like a walrus than Bette Midler. "It's Marty's first time in drag. Don't you think he's nervous enough without you being a total ass?"

"It's okay," Marty said, because he didn't want to instigate a battle to the death between the two brothers-in-law.

Kristin's father and uncle were already at each other's throats about some business deal gone bad. Jack was some kind of corporate big-wig. Marty never had been exactly clear on what the people in this family did for a living. Even Kristin's job mystified him. They all had corner offices and more vacation time than workdays. That's all Marty knew.

Tension weighed nearly as heavily on the air as the eyeliner Tyrone meticulously painted on his husband. Jonnie hadn't found his niche yet. He was trying out Liza this year. Some guys, like Tyrone and Jack, were showmen—dressed as women, dressed as men, didn't matter. Other guys were quiet, observant. That was Marty. He listened, he looked, and he could usually pull out the undercurrent of any situation. He and Jonnie had that much in common.

"Can I borrow your blusher?" George asked Jack.

Jack snapped, "No way. Get your own."

All at once, the tension burst and George hollered, "You think you know it all? Well, you don't know squat. You lost half a million in that—"

"It wasn't half a million," Jack cut in. "Nowhere near! And, hey, if you were a true drag queen instead of just a drama queen, maybe Tyrone wouldn't be so jealous every time you win this goddamn thing."

Jonnie stepped up and said, "My husband has every right to be jealous. He's got the looks, he's got the moves, and he's got legs. Why he hasn't won yet, I'll never understand."

George totally ignored Jonnie's plea, and turned back to Jack. "I'm taking you to court over that deal. It wasn't legit and you know it. You've pissed off a lot of investors, you self-righteous son of a bitch. First thing after the holiday, I'm getting the ball rolling on a class action."

Jack flipped on his long black Cher wig, then tossed his hair over both shoulders. Sucking in his cheeks, he said, "Go on and try, Georgie-Boy. You got nothing on me."

Marty couldn't stand the aggression. In his full-on *Vogue* outfit, he snuck away from the guest suite they were using as a dressing room. He couldn't see anyone in the hallway, thank goodness. All the women—Grandma Iris, Kristin and her mother Angela, George's wife Cynthia, plus Kristin's cousins Beth and Georgette—were downstairs munching on appetizers, waiting for the big show to begin.

A streak of nerves shot through Marty's belly, making his legs quiver. He thought about performing for Kristin's family. Oh God! Performing was not his thing. He was the kind of guy who felt nervous just placing an order at a restaurant. All eyes on him? It was too much pressure!

And dressed like this? Cone bra, cone hair, even a little cone codpiece to put over his white sequined bathing suit The cross-dressing didn't bother him, not with every Mayfair man taking part, but he didn't want Kristin's entire family staring at his winky-dink.

As Marty wandered down the hallowed halls of Mayfair Manor, he caught a whiff of something delicious. Turkey dinner was in the works, and Marty salivated as he imagined the delicious pies that would follow. Maybe they could skip the drag show and go straight to dessert?

Mmm... he could smell apples and cranberries among the hearty aromas of potatoes and stuffing, and he followed his nose toward the epicentre of aroma: the kitchen. Grandma Iris's cook, Brykia, went all out for the holidays. Marty couldn't resist grabbing a bite.

As he made his way toward the kitchen, Marty's thick nylons rubbed together. The soft shushing made him self-conscious, not just because of the sound but because that sheer fabric felt surprisingly good against his thighs. Sure he'd thought this family was kind of nutty when he'd first met them, but maybe the men were on to something. The drag show was truly carnivalesque, especially for an upper class bunch like the Mayfairs.

Marty slowed as he approached the kitchen. He felt a little weirded out by the prospect of Brykia seeing him dressed like Madonna, circa 1989.

He listened at the swinging saloon doors, too nervous to step inside.

He expected to hear pots clanging, but instead he heard the tippity-tap of high-heeled shoes. That was strange. Brykia always wore canvas runners. Must be someone else in the kitchen.

Suddenly Marty's fear of being seen and judged outweighed his hunger, and he rushed down the hall—well, as much as he could in heels. The guys had all put on pumps first thing, to get a feel for walking in them.

Some of the men were old hands with heels. Marty, not so much.

Chapter Two

By the time Marty returned the dressing room, the argument between Jack and George had died down. The atmosphere was still seething, though. The clouds of tension didn't break until Brykia knocked on the door a few minutes later.

"Madame Iris says the men must be fed," Brykia said as she wheeled a serving cart into the room. She laid out a cheese and fruit tray—standard fare at Mayfair family gatherings—and then handed George his own bowl of fruit, primarily red grapes. "Because of your lactose intolerance," she explained. "These ones never touched any cheese."

George grunted something that might have been a thank you, then tore the plastic wrap from his dish. Marty couldn't resist the brie with fig paste, and scarfed it down with enough bread to absorb the nerves boiling like acid in his belly.

For a while, everyone ate quietly. It made for a nice change. The room stayed pretty much silent until George let out a loud hissing noise. Marty turned just in time to see him brushing his arm against his flowing satin dress.

"You okay, Uncle George?"

George stared at his wrist, saying nothing. Whatever happened, he'd reacted with enough vigour to attract everyone's attention.

"What's wrong?" Jonnie asked.

"Nothing," George snapped, still staring at his arm. "Bug bite, maybe."

"I didn't think the great Mayfairs attracted pests," Tyrone teased.

"Jonnie attracted *you*, didn't he?" George shot back.

The room fell again into silence, but Marty felt that barb just as sharply as Tyrone must have. Even in marriage, guys like Tyrone and Marty would never be on equal footing with the Mayfair bloodline.

Jack and George fit in okay. They had that upper-class edge Marty would never understand, or even be able to copy. Kristin never made him feel like he was less worthy than the rich guys she'd dated before him, but her mother certainly did. So did Kristin's Aunt Cynthia, although Grandma Iris was the absolute worst. All she had to do was look at Marty to make him feel inferior.

It was a talent he hoped his wife would never develop.

All the men were sweating as show time approached, but none more profusely than George. Even through cake makeup, his face glowed red. Holy Moly, the guy was dripping like a faucet! Marty had no idea whether this was business as usual, since he'd never been backstage before. None of the other men seemed quite as nervous.

Downstairs, the women chanted: "On with the show! On with the show!"

God, was it really that time? Marty's stomach rumbled. Could he seriously lip-synch and strike a pose in front of his wife's family?

Ah, but he had to. No choice in the matter. It was a Mayfair family tradition.

Like ducks in a row, the men walked that green mile toward the front staircase, which was as grand as the Mayfair matriarch herself.

With the exceptions of George and Jonnie, the men seemed much more self-assured than Marty. Tyrone and Jack could walk in heels without stumbling, even when they started down the stairs.

Tyrone, as acting MC, led the line down to the luxurious marble foyer. The Mayfair women all wore their holiday best, which meant the best of the best: fine fabrics stitched with glass beads and crystals. From the Great Room, they cheered and hollered and snapped photographs of the men in drag.

The men's dresses were by far more showy and flamboyant than the women's, but they weren't quality pieces. Marty would hate to be sweating all over a three-thousand dollar Donna Karan. Not that Marty's perspiration held a candle to George's. The poor guy looked like a pig in a satin blanket.

"How you holding up?" Marty whispered as the other men paraded before their wives and family members.

The women cheered and applauded so loudly it was a challenge to catch George's answer. It sounded like, "A bit," but he was struggling for breath, like every inhale was a painful chore.

"Come on!" Tyrone hollered from the Great Room. "Hurry your sweet asses up!"

In that outfit, Tyrone didn't just look like Tina Turner, he *sounded* like Tina Turner, too! Ah, the power of suggestion!

The other men were way up ahead, strutting their stuff while Marty hung back in the marble foyer with George. George's illness was a happy excuse to delay entry into the Great Room, Marty had to admit. He hadn't even stepped off the stairs yet and, in truth, he felt too nervous to let go of the stair rail. The second he stepped onto that marble floor, he'd surely collapse. He'd put on the Spanx Tyrone had given him, but he felt bloated with bread and brie.

Why oh why had he eaten so much cheese?

He should have followed George's example and stuck to grapes!

"Happy Thanksgiving, Mayfair Ladies!"

Oh no, Tyrone was starting the show! Marty pressed his fake nails into the wooden railing so hard one of them flew right off, flipping in the air before click-clacking down on the marble.

Tyrone asked, "Are you ready for your men to put on a show?"

Hoots, hollers, applause!

Everyone but Marty had made it to the Great Room by now. Oh, except George. The poor old guy faced that direction, but wavered side to side like a buoy rocking on ocean waves.

"Your boys are dressed to impress," Tyrone went on. "Now, who's ready to rock?"

Laughter, wolf-whistles, cheers!

The longer Marty stared at the back of George's gleaming blonde wig, the more adamantly he felt that something must be wrong. That's when George started shaking, like he was having a seizure or something. Yeah, this was more than just stage fright or shoe troubles. His satin skirt quivered and quaked. His feather boa trembled like a squatting dog.

Tyrone clearly had no clue what was happening out in the hall. He announced, "Let me introduce them to you..."

George slid one foot forward on the marble, and it just kept going.

Marty had never seen such a large man do the splits. He belted with laughter, and clapped his hands to acknowledge the effort. "Way to go, man! That's quite a feat!"

When George made no response, Marty asked, "Hey, you okay, Uncle George? Need a hand?"

George fell to one side

In the next room, the Mayfair women cheered like crazy while Tyrone brought out the men in tights.

Marty tuned out the frenzy. Kicking off his heels, he raced across the foyer, falling so hard at George's side that he worried he'd put a hole in his nylons.

"George?" Marty smacked the guy's bloated face, but got no reaction. He shook George's shoulders hard enough that one fake boob rolled out the top of the big man's dress. "Quit fooling around, George!"

This fallen-over-splits position would be impossible for any out-of-shape man to hold for so long, unless he'd been training in the off-season. And training to hold his breath indefinitely, too.

"Guys!" Marty shouted. "Guys! I think you'd better come out here!"

Chapter Three

"Guys?" Marty cried. "Help!"

It grew apparent that nobody could hear him over Tyrone's introduction and the Mayfair women's frenzied cheers.

Marty tried slapping George in the face to revive him, but that didn't work. He tried shaking the guy, but George's head snapped back and forth in a way that did not look natural.

"Help!" Marty called out. "Kristin? Call an ambulance!"

He hadn't stopped shaking his new wife's uncle, and suddenly George's dead weight tumbled toward him. When the man's sweaty face landed against Marty's bare shoulder, that did it. He screamed in a way that was... let's just say less than manly. Okay, okay: he screamed like a scared little girl. And, in truth, with a man—a definitely dead man, he now realized—collapsed on his shoulder, who could blame him?

"What is the meaning of this?" Grandma Iris asked in a huff. "Young man, you are ruining the Amazing Annual Mayfair Family Drag Show!"

"Help!" Marty shouted, since he'd finally managed to grab their attention. "Help, please! I think he's dead!"

The magnitude of what was happening only really hit Marty when the family rushed into the marble foyer with a click-clack of heels.

Kristin pushed to the front of the crowd, and covered her mouth with both hands. "Marty, what happened?"

"I don't know!" His Spanx gripped his waistline so tight he could barely breathe. "It must have been a heart attack or something. He just collapsed like this."

"Doing the splits?" Kristin's mother, Angela, asked. "How bizarre. How very truly bizarre."

George's daughters fell at his sides. While they attempted to revive him in a whirlwind of chest punches and face slaps, Marty managed to shuffle toward the stairs.

The truth was obvious, at least to Marty. Uncle George was dead. No bringing him back.

The paramedics were called at Brykia's insistence. Like Marty, the sweet-faced cook couldn't understand her employer's desire to leave George's body in the foyer while they proceeded with their drag show. A death in the family should to take precedence over a stage performance. It would in any other household.

The Mayfairs were very strange people.

* * * *

Two paramedics in dark blue uniforms arrived on the scene at their leisure. When they entered the foyer of glitz and glam, one asked the other, "What the heck have we walked in on?"

Grandma Iris told them, "We were preparing for our annual drag show, and I dare say it would have gone off without a hitch if my wretched son-in-law didn't have the audacity to drop dead!"

The paramedics exchanged a dubious glance before checking for a pulse. The professionals agreed good old Uncle George was damaged beyond repair.

"But you called this in as a heart attack," said the short, shapely paramedic with the ponytail. "Doesn't look like a heart attack to me. See this mark here?"

The whole family crept closer to investigate the red spot on George's arm.

"Whatever is it?" Grandma Iris asked, clutching a lace hanky just beneath her lips. "Don't tell me he was killed by a pimple!"

"Not a pimple," said the other paramedic, who looked like a male Whoopie Goldberg. "Spider bite. Black widow, I'd say. Not that I'm an expert or anything, but I *did* minor in entomology back in college."

The ponytail paramedic perked up. "Hey, me too! Small world."

"Yes, yes, you two should get married some time," Cousin Beth snapped. "But before for you start planning the honeymoon, would you kindly explain how a black widow spider crawled all the way to our little corner of the planet and ended up on my father's arm?"

It was Beth's mother, Kristin's Aunt Cynthia, who answered that question. "I've heard news reports about dangerous spiders travelling here in bunches of grapes. By the time they end up in somebody's kitchen, they're so riled up they bite the first person they see!"

"Oh, so now you're an entomologist too?" Beth said to her mother—which, actually, struck Marty as a pretty rude way to talk to someone whose husband had just dropped dead.

Kristin's father jumped in to say, "No, no, Cynthia's right. We did have grapes earlier. Remember, guys? They were part of the cheese platter."

"And George had his own dish," Jonnie added. "Brykia wrapped it up for him—grapes that hadn't touched cheese."

"Because of his lactose intolerance," Tyrone said. With his hip popped and his knee bent, he looked exactly like Tina. Marty did so many double takes he thought he'd get whiplash.

"But I washed the grapes!" Brykia cried.

Marty jumped because he hadn't realized she was standing so close to him. In those rubber-soled shoes, the cook could sneak around like a ghost.

"I washed them, Madame Iris, I swear." Poor Brykia probably thought her job was in danger, and she was probably right, knowing what these Mayfairs were like. Brykia pleaded, "No spiders in the grapes. Everything was clean."

"Well, perhaps *your* clean and *my* clean are different cleans altogether," Grandma Iris replied.

"It doesn't matter where the spider came from," said Cousin Georgette. "Spider bites don't kill people. Daddy must have died of something else!"

"Oh, now you're an entomologist too?" Cousin Beth scoffed.

Georgette looked to the paramedics for answers. "Do spiders really kill people?"

"Not usually," both paramedics said at once. They blushed and both said, "You go," "No, you go," and then they laughed and blushed some more.

When her giggles died down, the ponytail paramedic said, "Death from spider bites are unusual unless the patient is quite old or quite young, or if their immune system is compromised in some way."

"Or," said the male Whoopie, "if the person doesn't seek immediate medical attention. He would have felt incredibly ill before he died."

Marty spoke up: "Yes, he was. I saw him. He was sweating like a pig!"

Male Whoopi asked, "What could have been so important that he'd risk his life by not going to the hospital?"

Tyrone looked at Jonnie, who looked at Jack, who flicked his long black hair behind his shoulders. "He'd never lost the drag competition."

The paramedics exchanged doubtful glances.

"It's a coveted title," Jack told them.

"Coveted enough *to die for*?" the paramedics asked, both at once. They quickly turned to each other and laughed. "Jinx! Buy me a Coke."

"You don't seem to be taking my uncle's death very seriously," Kristin said as she crossed the foyer to hold hands with her bereaved cousins.

"Well, there's nothing we can do to bring him back," said Ponytail Paramedic. "But, hey, I just got an idea!"

"I bet I know what it is," Male Whoopie replied.

They gazed deeply into each other's eyes like a couple of lovebirds.

Ponytail Paramedic said, "Guess. I bet you'll get it."

"I know I will. I can read your mind."

"Oh really?" Ponytail Paramedic's voice turned sultry and seductive when she said, "Well, then, tell me what I'm thinking right now."

Cousin Georgette rolled her eyes and said, "Ugh, get a room!"

Cousin Beth said, "No, first tell us what you were thinking."

"Oh." Male Whoopie turned away from Ponytail Paramedic just long enough to say, "We should call Professor Turquay to see if he can identify that bite. He knows everything there is to know about spiders

"Especially poisonous ones," Ponytail added.

"No," Aunt Cynthia cut in. Her voice sounded strangely hard and unemotional, considering her husband had just died. "No, that won't be necessary, thank you. Just take George away, to the morgue or wherever it is dead bodies go. Please."

The ponytailed paramedic took one step closer to the body, and cocked her head at Cynthia. "But Professor Turquay is a leading expert in sexual cannibalism."

"In *what*?" Kristin's mother cried.

"I should ask you to watch your language!" Grandma Iris added. "This is a respectable house."

"Black Widows are renowned for killing their mates," Whoopie explained. "The professor will be able to tell us if we're right about that bite, if it really was a Black Widow."

"No," Cynthia said sternly. Her hands formed fists at her sides. "This is all getting quite out of hand. Now take him away. Go!"

"It really is rather morbid," her daughter Georgette agreed. "Strange, though—Turquay. That name rings a bell."

"You're just hungry, dear," Grandma Iris consoled her granddaughter. "Come, let's return to the Great Room while these public servants clear the foyer of corpses."

Chapter Four

Beth and Georgette threw back their heads and wailed while Kristin escorted them from their father's bloated body. Everyone shadowed the young women, with Marty bringing up the rear. He followed the click-clack of high heels while Brykia trailed softly behind him.

"How are you holding up?" he asked her, since the Mayfairs' staff were usually easier to relate to than the Mayfairs themselves.

Brykia pouted, "My turkey will be black by the time this is over!"

While the paramedics clumsily attempted to un-split George's legs, Marty stared down at the man's sequined heels. That's when he remembered the noise he'd heard from the kitchen earlier on, when he'd swiftly escaped the dressing room.

Heels! He'd heard heels in the kitchen!

And that was just before Brykia brought up the cheese platter and George's guilty grapes. It hadn't been Brykia—she wore soft soles. So who was it?

Marty was getting a weird feeling about all this.

When he'd reached the Great Room, something came over him. He ran to the stage, grabbed Tyrone's microphone from its holder, and said, "I don't want to ruin Thanksgiving, but I think George was murdered!"

The family gasped. "Murdered? No! Never!"

Well, to be accurate, everyone but the Mayfair Matriarch gasped. Grandma Iris just sat there like a queen, looking all around with a quaint smile on her face.

From what Marty had heard on the family grapevine, Grandma Iris stood accused of slaughtering her share of husbands. But money erases all sins in these parts, and if there was one thing the Mayfairs had it was money.

"Marty, sit down!" Kristin shouted. "You're embarrassing yourself."

"No I'm not," Marty said as he tugged his vintage Madonna wedgie out of his butt crack. "There's something fishy going on here, and I don't want it swept under the rug."

"Hey, you weren't so keen to hit the stage," Jack piped up. With a cantankerous chuckle, Marty's father-in-law said, "Maybe *you* killed George so you wouldn't have to perform in the drag show. What's your alibi, kid?"

"Alibi for what?" Kristin's mother asked. "You heard the Ambulanciers. It was a spider bite, not a shot through the heart."

"Maybe it was a spider bite," Marty agreed, "but how, exactly, did a deadly spider get into George's grapes?"

Aunt Cynthia shook her head. "Weren't you listening? It's been all over the news: Black Widows get shipped north in bundles of grapes."

"But Brykia washed the grapes."

"And she did a bang-up job of it," Grandma Iris said, before issuing a dry Katherine Hepburn cackle.

Brykia brought out her rosary, pleading in silence as she joined Marty on the makeshift stage. He needed to convince the family she wasn't guilty, not even of being a bad grape-washer. The last thing he wanted was for Brykia to land the blame of Uncle George's death.

"Look," Marty said. "I saw George brush something off his arm when he was eating those grapes. I'm sure a spider *did* bite him, but I also suspect that spider was planted there... to kill him!"

The family gasped, and the grieving daughters sobbed on Kristin's shoulders.

"Brykia," Marty asked, "George's dish was covered in plastic wrap when you gave it to him. Why?"

The poor woman looked up from her beads, her eyes wide with alarm. She shook her head. "I don't know. I did not cover it. I...I..." Brykia burst into tears, hollering, "I did not kill him! I swear!"

"I know you didn't," Marty said, wrapping one arm around her.

"Ouch!" Brykia cried, pulling away from Marty's cone-bra. "Your bosoms are sharp enough to kill a man."

"Yeah," Jack said. "You were with George when he died, Marty. I'm still not convinced it wasn't you who did the dirty deed."

Marty was getting antsy in a He-Who-Smelt-It-Dealt-It sort of way. "I'm not the killer."

"Baby, we know. You wouldn't hurt a fly." Tyrone stood dramatically. In a classic *j'accuse* pose, he pointed at the man dressed as Cher. "You killed George, didn't you Jack?"

"I hardly think so," Jack said, brushing his long dark wig over both shoulders.

Jonnie picked that one up and ran with it. "Jack, you're the only one here with a motive. George was all twisted up about that business deal gone bad. He threatened to launch a class action suit after Thanksgiving."

"What happened?" Georgette asked Beth.

"Daddy lost money?" Beth asked Georgette.

"Girl, your daddy lost a buttload of cash," Tyrone answered. "And it was all Jack's fault. Jack has got to be the killer."

"I didn't kill anyone, you little puke! Jonnie, rein in your husband."

Jonnie waved a hand in the air. "Honey, I have triiied..."

"Marty, you were there when George threatened me," Jack called across the room. "Where would I have gotten a poisonous spider between then and the time Brykia handed him those grapes? I never even left the room!"

"That's right," Kristin's mom said, holding hands with her Cher-look-alike husband. "If anyone killed George, it was probably Tyrone."

"Oh, sure! Blame the black man! Real original, Angela."

Kristin's mother rolled her eyes dismissively, which pretty much said it all.

"I think what my wife is trying to say," Jack picked up, "is that George always took home your coveted Best in Show title."

Angela nodded decisively. "You'd have run over your own mother with a dump truck to get your hands on that prize."

Tyrone stamped his heel on the ground. "What'd you say about my mama?"

"My floors!" Grandma Iris cried. "How dare you!"

"I'm sorry, Granny, but you heard your daughter disrespecting my mama."

Iris turned decisively and said, "Angela, apologize to Tyrone."

"Mother, we're not children!"

"Angela!" she growled.

Lowering her gaze, Kristin's mother grunted, "I'm sorry, Tyrone."

He flicked his wig and shrugged. "Yeah, well, you really think I'm gonna kill my brother-in-law over some stupid drag contest?"

Grandma Iris's eyes flashed. She pounded her cane on her precious hardwood floor, then hoisted herself up. "The drag show is not stupid, Tyrone! It is a Mayfair family tradition! Now if you young people are quite done yammering, on with it! On with the show!"

"Grandma!" Georgette cried. "Daddy just died! They're not going to prance around the stage like a bunch of goofs."

"A bunch of goofs?" Iris replied. "No granddaughter of mine will refer to our men in skirts as a bunch of goofs!"

"Daddy died," Beth cut in. "The paramedics say a spider bite, Marty thinks it's murder. A stupid drag show should not be your top priority, Grandma, and I don't care if you cut me out of the will for saying so!"

"Insolent child," Iris grumbled.

"Crazy old lady," Beth shot back. "Somebody in this room probably killed my dad and you're hiding your head in the sand!"

Grandma Iris scoffed, "Nobody killed anybody, silly girl!"

With the tension coming to a head between grandmother and granddaughter, Marty lifted the microphone to his lips and said, "I witnessed it! I'm a witness!"

Chapter Five

The Mayfair family fell silent as Marty's voice echoed through the speakers.

"A witness?" Kristin asked. "A witness of what? What did you see, Marty?"

"Well, it's not so much what I saw," Marty replied, feeling less sure of himself now that all eyes were on him. "It's more like what I heard. I left the dressing room just before Brykia brought the grapes upstairs."

"Yeah, why did you leave?" Jack asked.

"To get away from you!" Marty wanted to say, but he was on thin ice already. What he actually said was, "I got nervous. Nervous-hungry, like when your stomach fills with acid and you need to eat some bread. So I went to grab something to eat, except I heard a noise in the kitchen: high heels."

"High heels?" Cynthia asked. "Well, so what? If you didn't actually see anything, you're not much of a witness."

Marty explained to the family, "I think whoever was clacking around the kitchen planted that spider in Uncle George's grapes. We're all wearing high heels—well, everyone except Brykia—so it could have been any one of us!"

"Could have been you," Jack shot back.

"Yeah, that's what I'm saying," Marty agreed. "I mean, it wasn't me, but it could have been."

"Well, it wasn't any of us men," Tyrone said, in a resonantly low tone of voice. "None of us left the holding room. We can all vouch for each other."

"Everyone but you," Jack heckled. "You're the only one who left the dressing room, Marty-Boy."

Marty swallowed hard. His heart thundered in his ears and his cone bra dug into his chest. He had no way of defending himself, except to say that he didn't do it and ask, "What about the women? You were all together down here, waiting for the show to start. Someone must have left the room at some point."

"We were all in and out," Grandma Iris said. "Powdering noses and such."

Scratching his head, Marty said, "There must be some way to figure this out. It couldn't have been an accident. I know in my gut Uncle George has been murdered. But whodunit?"

"Sit down, Marty," Kristin shouted across the room. She sounded exasperated. "Nobody dunit. Can't you see you're embarrassing yourself?"

"A true Mayfair would never accuse his fellow family members of murder," Grandma Iris clucked. "Not even if they were guilty!"

If Iris was trying to cast suspicion on herself, it was working.

"Brykia." Marty turned to the woman in the canvas shoes. "Who asked you to bring us the cheese platter up to us?"

"The lady of the house, of course."

"You mean Iris?"

A deep flush took over Brykia's cheeks and she looked down at her feet. "Yes."

Grandma Iris huffed and puffed and pounded her cane on the good hardwood floors. "You will not accuse me murder in my own home!"

Jack laughed. "Wouldn't be the first time."

Her elderly body shot arrow straight and her lips pursed, but it was Angela who defended the matriarch. "My mother is not a man-killer."

"No, just a ball-breaker," Tyrone chuckled.

Jonnie's body tensed, and he took his turn. "Marty, look, I appreciate what you're trying to do, here, but my mother's not a murderer and neither is anyone else in this family. George got bit by a spider and he didn't call an ambulance. He died for drag. Simple as that."

"I think I'm starting to agree with Jonnie," Cousin Beth said, her cheeks streaked with tears. "Anyway, we'll know more when Professor Turquay gets here. He'll be able to tell us what kind of spider bit Daddy."

Suddenly, Cousin Georgette shot up from the couch and shouted, "Turquay! T-U-R-Q-U-A-Y!"

Everyone turned to look at her.

"I knew I'd seen that name somewhere. It was spelled funny and it made me laugh." Georgette turned to her mother, and her face fell with an expression of deep shock.

"What's wrong?" Marty asked. "Where did you see the professor's name?"

"It was on that shipping box when we got here," Georgette murmured. "Remember, Mother? It was on that package from the university."

Cynthia waved a dismissive hand in her daughter's direction. "I don't know what you're talking about, child. What shipping box?"

"It was addressed to you," Georgette went on. "Sent here care of Grandmama. I asked what was in it, but you didn't answer. You just picked it up and took it away…"

"I saw that box too," Beth said, quietly, like she was in a trance. "It had one of those 'live animal' stickers on it. I was about to ask what it was when Grandmother yanked me into the front room and called for tea."

"The spider!" Tyrone gasped, covering his pink lips with bright purple fingernails.

"Where?" Jack squealed, jumping onto the nearest chair.

Tyrone tsked. "Not in here. In the box! The live animal box. Honey, keep up. We ain't slowin' down for y'all."

"Mother!" Beth cried.

But Tyrone obviously craved his moment in the sun, because he stood and pointed an accusing finger at Cynthia, and said, "Honey, you killed your husband."

Cynthia's eyes filled with tears, but she blinked them away. "Well, that's the silliest thing I've ever heard! Me, kill my husband? Why-ever would I do such a thing?"

"Money?" Tyrone asked. "Rich man like that'd probably leave his wife a tidy sum."

"Maybe he was cheating on you," Marty proposed.

"Or because he looks better in a dress than you!" Jonnie said.

"Don't be vile," Cynthia replied. "George always looked atrocious in women's wear. How he managed to win the drag competition year after year, I'll never..." Her lip began to quiver as she said, "...I'll never know."

Georgette stroked her mother's back. "Daddy was funny on stage. That's why everybody voted for him. He made us all laugh."

"That's right," Kristin and her mother both said.

Jack relented. "We'll all miss the guy's drag performance. I can't deny that."

Cynthia's stiff upper lip broke and she wailed as she said, "It wasn't my idea!"

"What wasn't your idea?" Marty asked into the microphone.

"It was Mother! Mother insisted! She said I had to carry on the Mayfair family tradition!"

"Hush, Cynthia," Grandma Iris chastised.

"What Mayfair family tradition?" Marty asked. "You mean the drag show?"

"No," Cynthia sobbed. "There's another one, an older one... one you men don't find out about... until it's too late!"

Chapter Six

"We will have no more of this nonsense," Iris growled.

"It's true!" Cynthia sobbed into her hanky. "Mother said it's what all Mayfair women did, husband after husband. She did it, her mother did it, just like her mother before her. They all murdered their men."

"*What*?" Jack and Tyrone shrieked.

Grandma Iris covered her face with one hand. "Oh, Cynthia, you silly, stupid girl"

"This is too... weird," Georgette said.

"Mom, you didn't really?" Beth whispered. "You didn't do it."

"I did!" Cynthia wept. "Your grandmother bought a special kind of spider from the man at the university—a black widow bred to be vicious and very, very poisonous. She told me all I had to do was get Brykia out of the kitchen long enough to put it in George's grapes, and it would be easy enough to explain away."

Everyone turned to Brykia, who seemed confounded for a moment, and then said, "That's right! Madame Cynthia asked me to find her a jar of beets from the cellar. I left her alone in the kitchen."

"And that's whose heels I heard clacking!" Marty said.

"Yes, it's true," Cynthia admitted. "Cart me off to prison. I deserve to be thrown in a dungeon for the rest of my day, nothing but bread and water to sustain me!"

"Certainly not," Grandma Iris growled. "I should say, not until after we've all enjoyed Brykia's wonderful turkey. And we won't be starting dinner until after the Amazing Annual Mayfair Family Drag Show!"

Everybody groaned, and the grieving daughters tried their best to explain why, this year, the Mayfairs should give the drag show a miss.

Meanwhile, Brykia fled to the kitchen to tend to the bird and probably start searching for a job in a house without a longstanding tradition of murder.

Kristin joined Marty on stage, beaming proudly as she approached him. Removing the microphone from his hand, she switched it off and replaced it on the stand. Then she kissed him on the cheek and said, "I'm very proud of you."

"Proud enough to swear you won't murder me?"

"Cross my heart."

"Even if your mom says you have to?"

"Since when do I listen to my mother?" Kristin asked. "She told me not to marry you, and I married you anyway."

Marty sagged. "Angela said that? I thought she liked me, at least a little bit."

Taking his hand, Kristin said, "Maybe that's why she didn't want me marrying you—because one day I'd have to kill you."

"Do you think your mom knew about this Mayfair Family Tradition?"

Kristin shivered. "I hope not. I sure didn't."

She helped him cross the stage in heels, and then held his hand tight as they stepped down the three stairs to the floor.

"You can take off those heels now," Kristin said. "I really don't think the show's going to happen."

Marty shrugged. "It's okay. I need the practice for next year. With Uncle George gone, it's anyone's game."

Kristin, rolled her eyes, but smiled. "Come on. Let's tell those paramedics what happened. Maybe they know when the police will get here."

But when they stepped into the huge marble foyer, the paramedics were nowhere to be seen.

"Maybe they went out to the ambulance," Kristin said.

Just then, they heard a distinctly suspicious giggle from the closet.

Marty marched over to it, which was no easy feat in his high-heeled shoes, and yanked the door open.

Inside, Male Whoopie's fingers were bunched up in his partner's ponytail. She was tugging on his dreads while they smooched like they'd both spent the last decade on a desert island.

Marty cleared his throat, and they both jumped. Looking guilty and shocked, they stammered, "Oh, we were just... clues, looking for... clues..."

"In each other's pants?" Kristin asked.

The paramedics blushed and apologized, but Marty actually thought it was pretty cute.

"We just wanted to tell you we know who killed George," Marty said. "His wife is the culprit. It's a long story."

"Well, she can tell it to the cops," Male Whoopi replied. "Sorry, that sounded meaner than I meant it. The police are on their way, is what I should have said, so she can give them her full confession when they arrive."

They stood awkwardly inside the closet, until, finally, Kristin wished them a happy Thanksgiving and shut the door so they could get back to... looking for clues...

"Well, this has sure been an eventful Thanksgiving," Marty said.

"And we haven't even eaten yet."

As his new wife squeezed his hand lovingly, Marty listened to the Mayfair family sobbing, screaming and arguing in the next room. Through it all, he'd nearly forgotten he was wearing his Madonna outfit. The bodysuit and stocking had become a second skin while they were busy solving George's murder. Even the heavy blonde wig wasn't feeling too cumbersome. The heels would still take a bit of practice, though.

"We've got leftovers in the fridge at home," Kristin said. "Are you married to the idea of a big family dinner with the Mayfairs?"

"I'm only married to one Mayfair," Marty teased. "And if she's ready to go, so am I. Let me just change out of this Madonna get-up."

As he kicked off his shoes, Kristin asked, "Which one of you killed the spider?"

Marty froze at the bottom of the stairs.

"The black widow," Kristin continued. "It bit Uncle George. Did he kill it?"

Marty started to tremble. "No, I don't think so. I saw him brush his arm against his skirt, but... Holy Moly, the spider must still be up there!"

As Marty raced out the front door, Kristin followed behind. "You're just going to leave your clothes here?"

"Burn them!" he said.

"We're going to drive all the way home with you dressed like Madonna?"

"Beats getting bit by a black widow," Marty squealed. "Anyway, men dressing like women is your family's proudest tradition!"

Getting her keys out of her purse, Kristin said, "So is murder, apparently."

Hopefully this Thanksgiving spelled an end to *that* Mayfair family tradition. But as Marty took off his wig and tucked into the car, he felt kind of disappointed that he did all that rehearsing for the drag competition and now he'd never get to show off his moves. Maybe when they got home, he'd put on a private showing for Kristin. She'd like that.

Murder, he could do without. But the other Mayfair family tradition, the one that involved a lip-synch competition, back-breaking choreography, and larger-than-life glam? Well, he hoped the Mayfair men would hold on to that.

The End

~

Thanks for reading **Queer and Cozy Mysteries**! If you enjoyed this compilation, why not leave a quick review? Reviews help other readers find the stories they're looking for while avoiding books that may not suit their tastes.

Happy reading and have a great day!
~J.J. Brass

Don't miss out!

Visit the website below and you can sign up to receive emails whenever J.J. Brass publishes a new book. There's no charge and no obligation.

https://books2read.com/r/B-A-GBNC-TFAO

BOOKS 2 READ

Connecting independent readers to independent writers.

Lightning Source UK Ltd.
Milton Keynes UK
UKHW021131140722
405856UK00009B/2219